J.M.

Mary E. Pearce, a Londoner by birth, now lives in the relative peace of Gloucestershire. She tackled various jobs – shop assistant, filing clerk, waitress, usherette – before settling down to write seriously in the 1960s. Her career began with the appearance of short stories in magazines and has led, with the publication of six novels, to her present success.

D1324724

Also by Mary E. Pearce

THE APPLE TREE SAGA:

APPLE TREE LEAN DOWN
THE SORROWING WIND
JACK MERRYBRIGHT

CAST A LONG SHADOW
THE LAND ENDURES
SEEDTIME AND HARVEST
POLSINNEY HARBOUR

MARY E. PEARCE

The Two Farms

Futura

A *Futura* Book

Copyright © Mary E. Pearce 1985

First published in Great Britain in 1985 by
Macdonald & Co (Publishers) Ltd
London & Sydney

This Futura edition published in 1986

All rights reserved.
No part of this publication may be reproduced,
stored in a retrieval system, or transmitted, in any
form or by any means without the prior
permission in writing of the publisher, nor be
otherwise circulated in any form of binding or
cover other than that in which it is published and
without a similar condition including this
condition being imposed on the subsequent
purchaser.

*All characters in this publication are fictitious and any resemblance
to real persons, living or dead, is purely coincidental.*

ISBN 0 7088 3140 0

Reproduced, printed and bound in Great Britain by
Hazell Watson & Viney Limited,
Member of the BPCC Group,
Aylesbury, Bucks

Futura Publications
A Division of
Macdonald & Co (Publishers) Ltd
Greater London House
Hampstead Road
London NW1 7QX
A BPCC plc Company

For Margaret Peach

Chapter One

The valley ran from north to south and the two farms, Godsakes and Peele, lay on opposite sides of it. The Suttons had been tenants at Peele for four generations, having come there in 1746, but the Riddlers had been at Godsakes only since 1821. The little valley was sheltered and warm and the land was as rich and fertile as any land in Gloucestershire, varying from a light sandy loam in the upper part of the valley to a rich red marl in the lower parts. On the same side of the valley as Godsakes, lying in a hollow beside it, was a third farm known as Granger's, but it was only sixty acres or so and all of it heavy clay.

Peele, on the valley's eastern slopes, was sheltered by the round green hill known locally as Luton Camp, while Godsakes, on the western side, had its back to the twin humps of Hogden Hill and Derritt Hill. On both these farms the fields sloped gently down to the flat green valley floor where the Timmy Brook, with many a twist, made its way through the meadows to join the little River Cran outside the hamlet of Abbot's Lyall.

In summer the Timmy Brook flowed sedately between its banks but every winter without fail it would flood out over the meadows, turning the valley into a lake, sometimes for two or three weeks at a time. This flooding, although it caused problems, was welcomed by the valley farmers, for it left the meadows so enriched that in spring they gave new grass for the cows three weeks before it grew elsewhere. These meadows were common land and, except at haymaking time, stock from all three farms grazed there together, crossing and re-crossing the brook by a number of little bridges set between the steep banks.

7

John Sutton of Peele Farm, with four generations of breeding behind him, was a man of some education and polish. He was also a vigorous, go-ahead man who farmed his land by modern ideas. Isaac Riddler, on the other hand, was a near-illiterate cattle dealer who, after years of scrimping and saving, had taken the tenancy of Godsakes with more courage than capital. His son Morris had succeeded him but farmed in the same haphazard way and was almost always behind with his work. It was inevitable, therefore, that the educated John Sutton, successfully farming three hundred acres, should feel himself superior to the uncouth Morris Riddler, muddling along on his hundred and ten.

Still, they were good enough neighbours until, in 1842, their landlord, James Goodwin of Allern Hall, finding himself in need of money, decided to sell the three valley farms lying so far from the main estate, and offered the tenants first refusal. The estate agent, Mr Maule, called on John Sutton first; he stated the exact terms of the offer and gave him a week to think it over.

'Then I would be much obliged if you would come and see me and let me know your decision.'

Sutton did not need to think. He knew his own mind. And the agent had no sooner gone than he was striding his well-kept fields, already seeing them as his own, already busy making plans. The purchase presented no financial problem because only two years before an elderly uncle, formerly a hop merchant, had died leaving Sutton a tidy fortune. In fact the chance of buying Peele so accorded with his ambitions that it seemed like the answer to a half-formed prayer.

For Riddler, however, it was a different matter. The agent's news came as a shock.

'Buy Godsakes? How much?' he asked.

'Mr Goodwin would accept eighteen pounds per acre for the farm itself and fifty shillings per acre for the hill pastures.'

'But that would be over two thousand pounds! I haven't got it!' Riddler said.

'It would fetch more than that if it went for auction. It really is an excellent farm, with the common rights on the meadows as well, and I'm sure if you were to try the bank they would be only too happy to advance whatever sum you need.'

'Yes, at an interest of four per cent!'

'Does that mean you do not wish to buy?'

'Dammit! Don't I get time to think?'

'Yes, of course,' the agent said. 'You have until a week today. Then I would like you to call on me and let me know your decision.'

'You're in a hurry, aren't you? We're in the middle of haymaking here.'

But although he wanted time to think, Riddler too had made up his mind, for he saw that the chance was too good to miss. And the risk of borrowing from the bank, although it worried him at first, soon came to seem trivial compared with the richness of the reward. He talked about it to his wife, Agnes.

'Well, for one thing, we don't want to leave here, do we, when we've been here twenty-one years and put so much work into the place? We don't want to have to start again in a strange new place, do we, eh?'

He was also thinking of his son, Eddy, at that time nine years old.

'What a wonderful thing it'll be for him – taking over a farm of his very own! We shall never have such a chance again. Not at that price. It's too good to miss.'

'How much will you have to borrow?'

'I reckon about six hundred pounds.'

'You'll see Mr Maule, then?'

'Be sure I shall!'

But the whole week went by and Riddler, behindhand as usual, was still at work down in the meadows, anxious to get his hay carted before a threatened break in the weather. Mr Maule would have to wait. There was no great hurry, he told himself. It would do him no harm to stew for a while.

John Sutton's purchase of his farm was already under way by

this time. An agreement had been signed between the two parties and ten per cent of the purchase price had been deposited with the estate lawyers.

'What about Hessey at Granger's? Have you had his answer yet?'

'Yes, he's decided not to buy. Hardly surprising, really, seeing he's in his seventies and has no sons to come after him.' The agent met John Sutton's gaze. 'Would you be interested?'

'Yes, I would. But that's a clay farm. Sumpy. Bad. It would need a great deal doing to it.'

'Mr Goodwin would accept fifteen pounds the acre.'

'I am willing to pay that.'

'Excellent. I thought you might.'

'What about Riddler at Godsakes? Will he be buying?' Sutton asked.

'He hasn't given his answer yet but it seems very doubtful,' the agent said. 'Not much capital there, I think, and he seems nervous of borrowing. I got the impression he wouldn't buy.'

'Well, if he doesn't, you know where to come – I'll have it off you like a shot.'

'That would give you quite a substantial holding,' the agent said with a little smile.

'It would mean the whole valley was mine,' Sutton said. 'I've been thinking about it a lot and the idea has taken hold of me. Riddler is a good enough chap but he's forty years behind the times. A glance over Godsakes shows you that. I could farm it a lot better than he does, and once I've got Granger's put to rights, every acre in that valley would be farmed right to the top of its bent.'

'Well, I'll give Riddler another few days, then I'll go over and chivvy him up. But I don't think you need worry. I would say Godsakes is as good as yours.'

Sutton nodded as though satisfied but when the agent was seeing him off he brought the subject up again. 'If Godsakes went to auction, how much do you think it would fetch?'

'I would think, perhaps, three thousand pounds.'

'Yes, well,' Sutton said, 'certainly if I were there, I would be willing to bid that high.'

The agent smiled understandingly.

'I'll see Riddler as soon as I can.'

'What the hell do you mean, Sutton's made you a better offer? Tenants had first option, you said, and *I'm* the tenant here, don't forget.'

'You seemed doubtful about buying.'

'I wanted time to think, that's all.'

'Quite so,' the agent said. 'But I asked for your answer within a week and it is now eleven days since we talked.'

'I don't sit around on my arse here, you know! I have got my day's work to do –'

'And I have mine.'

'Yesterday I went into town and had a talk with Mr Forester at the bank. I was getting it all fixed up, finding out how I was placed. I told him the price I'd got to pay and he said there was no problem at all. Two thousand, one hundred and eighty pounds. That's the price you set on this farm and you've got no right to welsh on me.'

'If you had come when I asked you to, the matter would have been settled by now, but I have my employer's interest to think of, and in view of Mr Sutton's offer –'

'What *is* his offer?' Riddler asked. 'Thirty pieces of silver, is it?'

'Three thousand pounds,' the agent said.

'And what if I say I'll pay that? Will you stick to the price this time or will you go running over to Peele to see if Sutton will bid higher still?'

'If you're prepared to pay three thousand pounds –'

'I've said so, haven't I?' Riddler snarled.

'Then I shall go back to Mr Goodwin and apprise him of the fact. I can't make any promise, of course, but if I advise him to accept he will most probably do so.'

'Then for God's sake get on with it,' Riddler said, 'and get the lawyers to tie it up.'

In due course the transaction was made and he became the owner of Godsakes Farm. But to do so he had to borrow fourteen hundred pounds from the bank, more than twice what he'd bargained for, and he never forgave John Sutton for that. The old neighbourliness was gone, and a bitter hatred took its place. He always tried to avoid Sutton now but in the Corn Hall one market day they came face to face by accident. The story of their quarrel was well known and the meeting was watched with interest all round and Riddler, being aware of this, stood four-square in front of Sutton and in a loud voice said:

'I would turn my back on this man – except that he'd stick a knife in it!'

John Sutton looked at him with a mixture of tolerance and contempt. 'You don't seem to understand – farming is a business, like any other, and in business there's always competition.'

'Well, in this competition you lost, didn't you?'

'Just for the present, yes, perhaps.'

'What the hell do you mean by that?'

'Farming is not quite the same as it was. Things are progressing. There's change in the air. And you will have to farm a sight more efficiently than you have done till now if you are to keep abreast of the times and pay off the mortgage loan you've been foolish enough to saddle yourself with.'

'I'll pay it off, be sure of that!'

'Well, we shall see,' Sutton said.

In the summer of 1843 the well in the farmyard at Godsakes ran dry. This had never happened before and Riddler knew who was to blame: John Sutton, taking over Granger's Farm in the clay hollow just below, had had the land drained to a depth of six feet or more and this had drawn off the underground springs that had fed the well at Godsakes.

Riddler got on his horse at once and rode into Missenham to seek his solicitor's advice. But it was a question, Mr Nicholson said, of *damnum absque injuria*, or 'damage without wrong'.

'In other words, Mr Riddler, your neighbour has a perfect

right to drain his own land if he so wishes, just as you have a right to drain yours, and if it causes damage to some other party, I'm afraid there is no redress for it.'

A piece of legal information which cost Riddler half a guinea.

'Why is it that the blasted law is always on the side of the scoundrels?' he asked his wife when he got home.

The shortage of water was acute. It had to be carried up from the brook. And Riddler had no choice but to sink a deeper well. It was yet another expense he could ill afford; yet another setback to be laid at John Sutton's door; and in its wake, over the years, one misfortune succeeded another until, as Agnes Riddler said, it seemed that the farm had a curse on it. First it was a bout of quarter-ill, which took three of their best cows; then it was the failure of the corn harvest; and then, in 1844, winter gales tore the roof from one of the older cattle-sheds.

None of these misfortunes was ever visited on Peele. There, obviously, everything prospered and Sutton, now that he owned the farm, was making improvements everywhere. Hedges had been grubbed up, throwing two or three fields into one; new farm buildings had been built to house the most modern machinery; and more grassland was being ploughed to grow more corn.

He had also built himself a new house, up on a gentle slope of land just below the beechwoods, set at a slight angle to give a view southwards along the valley. It was a fine square-built house of cream-coloured stucco finish and in front of it lay a gravel drive, a garden laid out with trees and shrubs, and a lawn running down to a small lake. The old farmhouse was occupied by the bailiff now and a row of conifers had been planted to screen it, and the farm buildings, from the windows of the new house.

Riddler would look across the valley and sneer at John Sutton's pretensions.

'He fancies himself as some sort of squire,' he would say to his wife and children, and he called Sutton 'the Marquis of Peele'.

Certainly the new house at Peele was a very handsome residence and drew the attention of anyone travelling along the

13

valley road. The old house at Godsakes, on the other hand, built of locally quarried stone, so merged with its background of fields that had it not been for the pale sandy track climbing the side of the valley towards it, people would scarcely have known it was there.

'What a contrast between the two farms,' visitors to Peele would say, and even those who knew nothing of farming could see that Godsakes was badly run-down.

Riddler, having cut down on labour, was now working harder than ever, hoping to make up for it, but often while he ploughed in one field his two men, Lovell and Smith, would be taking it easy in another. Sometimes he would steal up on them and bawl at them over the gate, but it made little impression on them. They would plod all the way across the field just to ask him what he had said. They had no respect for him nowadays and behind his back they called him 'Mo'. Sometimes, on market days, Riddler was inclined to drink too much and in the morning he would have a thick head.

'Old Mo's been at it again,' Bob Lovell would say to Nahum Smith. 'We shan't get much sense out of him today.'

They argued with him constantly over the work that had to be done and he was too easily overborne.

'No good cutting that hay today, master. There's rain in the offing as sure as fate.'

After four dry days, Riddler, cursing and swearing at them, gave orders that the hay was to be cut. There followed a week of heavy showers and the hay was more than half spoilt.

It was the same with everything. The farm-work was always in arrears. Once they were so late sowing their spring corn that it never ripened properly and Riddler fed it green to the stock. One heifer died of it and a number of ewes slinked their lambs. Stock was down to a minimum now and the lack of manure showed itself in crops of sickly looking kale and mangolds no bigger than a woman's fist. In the autumn of 1844 Riddler found he could not afford to buy seed corn and some of his fields, left unploughed, tumbled down to grass and weeds.

14

John Sutton, across the valley, could see how bad things were at Godsakes and one afternoon he rode over, coming straight into the field where Riddler was flattening mole-hills.

'It's two years since you bought this farm and if you've got any sense you'll admit that you're just about done for. I don't care to see a good farm going to ruin like this and I am willing to pay you exactly the sum you gave for it. No one else would pay you that. Not in the state it's in today. So why not sell out to me before you're dragged down deeper still?'

Riddler, in shirtsleeves, a heavy mattock in his hands, looked up at Sutton on his horse and gave a deep-throated growl.

'Get off my land,' he said savagely.

Later, at tea with his family, he talked about Sutton's visit.

'My father slaved all his life, scraping enough money together to take this farm for himself and me. He loved this place . . . The valley, the hills, the meadows down there and the Timmy Brook. He slaved his guts out to get this land and I'm damned if I'll ever let it go.'

'We are still slaving,' Agnes said, 'and where will it get us in the end?'

'Things'll get better, you'll see. I've been making a lot of mistakes and that loan is putting a strain on us. We've had bad luck these past two years but things will pick up for us from now on. I promise you that.'

'Why not sell while the price is still good? Sutton means to have this place and he will do sooner or later, I'm sure, being the kind of man he is.'

'Is that all you can say to me? Is that your way of cheering me up?' Riddler's voice, always loud, now rose to an angry shout. 'Christ Almighty!' he exclaimed. 'Things've come to a pretty pass when my own wife wants to do me down. You talk about slaving? Hell's bells! At least you slept in your bed last night! *I* didn't. Oh, no, not me! I was up with a sick cow – '

'Please don't shout at me,' Agnes said. 'I know how hard you have to work.'

Riddler fell silent, staring at her, his anger gradually dying

15

down. Then, as he spooned buttered beans into his mouth, he turned to look at his two children.

'Mother works hard, too,' Kirren said.

'Yes, I know she does,' Riddler said.

'She works just as hard as you ever do. You've got no right to shout at her.'

'All right, all right, that's enough,' Riddler said.

Kirren, although she was only eight always had more to say for herself than her brother, Eddy, who was twelve. And often when she looked at her father, her eyes were darkly hostile.

'Mother isn't well,' she said. 'You ought not to make her work so hard.'

'Not well? Not well? Who says she's not well?'

'Mrs Lovell and Mrs Smith.'

'Kirren, be quiet,' Agnes said.

'What's this about you not being well?'

'Nothing, Morris. Nothing at all. I get a bit tired sometimes, that's all, and I worry about you working so hard. That's why I thought if you gave up the farm – '

'I'm not giving up and that's flat!' Riddler said. 'Neither John Sutton nor anyone else is taking this farm away from me and you'd better make up your mind to it!'

Outside in the foldyard afterwards Riddler talked to his young son.

'Women are different from us, somehow. They don't seem to see things the same way at all. But you understand, don't you, boy? You wouldn't want me to let the farm go any more than I would myself?'

'No, father,' Eddy said, 'especially not to Mr Sutton, after what he did to you.'

Riddler was much moved by this. He gripped Eddy's shoulder and gave it a squeeze.

'Sutton won't have it, I'll see to that. I swear to it by Almighty God. I'm going to make a few changes here, get things back on an even keel. I only need a bit of luck and now that you are leaving school and will be doing a full day's work – '

'I shall work hard, father, cross my heart.'

'I know you will. I know it fine. You're worth two of Lovell

16

and Smith and if we put our backs into it we shall soon pull the place up, shan't we, eh? Oh, we shall show them a thing or two, you and me! We'll make them sit up. We shall, that's a fact!'

Riddler's son was his pride and joy; his hope for the future; his bright star. He saw the boy as a young man – clever, determined, vigorous, strong. Eddy had qualities he himself lacked and in a few years' time he would be making the old place hum. Riddler saw it as plain as glass and the happy vision made him smile.

But this dream, like so many others, was to be most cruelly shattered, for that winter an epidemic of influenza swept through Gloucestershire, and Riddler's family went down with it. His wife and daughter soon recovered but Eddy developed pneumonia and in three weeks he was dead.

Riddler was beside himself with grief. For days he hardly spoke at all but went about his work in an anguished trance. Often he failed to come in for his meals and Agnes would have to go out to him and plead with him to come in and eat. Once she found him in tears in the barn and when she touched him on the shoulder he burst out at her in a terrible howl:

'Why did it have to be the boy that died?'

Agnes turned and left him and outside in the yard came upon her daughter, Kirren, standing like a small statue, an empty bucket in each hand. The child's face was pale and stiff. Agnes saw that she had heard.

'Your father is not himself,' she said. 'He doesn't know what he's saying. We must both try to be patient with him.'

Kirren said not a single word; only stared at her mother with darkened eyes and then, with the ghost of a shrug, turned away towards the pump.

Chapter Two

John Sutton was a widower, his wife having died in 1832, giving birth to their only child, a son named Philip. Sometimes Sutton worried about this son of his, brought up in a household run by an elderly housekeeper without other children for company, but in the winter of 1844 this problem unexpectedly solved itself.

The weather was bad in December and one black wet night just after Christmas a drover driving a large flock of sheep through the valley stopped at Peele asking if he could sleep in a barn and leave his flock to graze in the meadows before moving on in the morning. The bailiff, Warren Oakley, gave permission, but he never learnt the man's name, nor did he see his face clearly, and in the morning, before it grew light, the drover and his flock had gone.

Nothing more was thought of it then; the man had given no trouble whatever; but three days after he had gone a small boy in ragged clothes was caught stealing turnips from a field and told the bailiff that his uncle, the drover, had left him behind deliberately, telling him to lie low and not leave the barn for two or three days. Oakley brought the boy to the house and John Sutton questioned him.

'Do you mean to tell me that you've been in the barn since Thursday night?'

The boy gave a nod.

'Weren't you cold?'

Another nod.

'What is your name?'

'Jim,' the boy said, and gave a small, husky cough, partly from fear and partly from cold.

'Jim what?' Sutton asked.

This time the boy shook his head.

'Well, then, what is your uncle's name?'

Yet another shake of the head.

'Do you mean you don't know or have you been told not to tell?'

'Uncle said not to tell. He said he'd put a curse on me and if I told I should fall down dead.'

'What else did your uncle say?'

'He said for me to stop in the barn and keep out of sight for two or three days. Then to go to the nearest workhouse and ask for them to take me in.'

'Have you no parents?'

'No. They're dead.'

'Where was your home before they died?'

'I don't remember. It's too far back.'

The boy was about ten years old, dirty, louse-ridden, dressed in rags, and with red scurfy sores on his face and neck. He also had a large bruise just below his left eye and a smaller bruise on his upper lip.

'Did your uncle do that to you?'

'Yes.'

'Does he often beat you?'

'Yes, when he's drunk. He doesn't like me. He says I smell.'

'And whose fault is that, I'd like to know? Why, if I had that blackguard here now –'

Sutton was fond of children and the boy's condition angered him. He turned towards the farm bailiff.

'All right, Oakley, you can go. I'll keep the boy here for a day or two while I decide what to do with him. Come along with me, Jim, and we'll see if Mrs Abelard can find you something better to eat than a raw turnip out of the field.'

The housekeeper was none too pleased at having a dirty, verminous child presented to her in her clean kitchen and she told Sutton so in vigorous terms.

'The boy is starving,' Sutton said. 'Give him some good hot food to eat, then get him washed and into clean clothes.'

'What clean clothes?' Mrs Abelard asked. 'Has he brought his valise with him?'

'Some old clothes of Philip's, of course, what else?'

'And what shall I do with him after that?'

'Philip will be back by then. He's gone for a ride with Charlie Clements. He can take young Jim under his wing.'

'Do you mean he's to stop in the house? Sleep in one of our nice clean beds?'

'Yes, of course. Why shouldn't he?'

'And how long for?' Mrs Abelard asked, scandalized at the prospect.

'As to that, I have no idea. We shall just have to see,' Sutton said.

By the time Philip came in Jim had been so thoroughly scrubbed that his fair skin glowed as though lit from within, and, dressed in borrowed velveteens, with his fair hair brushed smoothly down, looked presentable enough, though Philip made a face of distaste at sight of the red sores on his skin.

'What's that? Is it leprosy?'

'Of course it isn't,' Mrs Abelard said. 'Soap and water will cure that – if he stops in this house long enough.'

'What's his name?'

'Jim, he says.'

'Where has he come from? Why is he here?'

'Don't ask me!' Mrs Abelard said. 'Ask your father, standing there.'

John Sutton told Jim's story to his son. 'He's going to stay with us at present, while I make certain enquiries and see if his uncle can be traced. But unless young Jim agrees to tell us his name I don't hold out much hope. At present he refuses to say.'

'Refuses to tell us his name?' Philip said. 'Hah! *I'll* soon get it out of him!'

'Yes, well, maybe you will. Take him out with you, anyway, and show him the farm. Take him to see that new pony of yours. He'll like that, won't you, Jim?'

The two boys went out together and were gone until darkness fell. They then returned to the house and had tea with Mrs Abelard and the maid, Alice, at the kitchen table in front of the fire.

'Well, then, Master Philip, did you get him to tell you his name?'

'No, not yet, but I will!' Philip said.

During the next three weeks the boys were together a great deal, mostly out and about in the fields, for the farm stock, especially the sheep, drew Jim like a magnet. And Philip, during this time, would question him repeatedly, trying to make him reveal his name.

'Is it Smith? Is it Brown? Is it Murgatroyd?'

Jim only shook his head but the name Murgatroyd made him smile.

'That's it! That's it!' Philip cried. 'His name is Murgatroyd! I know it is!'

'No, it isn't.'

'What is it, then?'

'My uncle told me not to tell.'

'Well, you're not going to be called Sutton, so there, and you needn't think it!' Philip said.

One day when Jim was out with the flock, talking to the shepherd, George Abelard, Philip came running up the field in a state of great excitement.

'Jim! You're wanted up at the house. It seems your uncle has come back for you.'

Jim's face went dreadfully white and he stood as though turned to stone. Then, suddenly, Philip laughed.

'I was only teasing you! Lord, if you could've seen your face! I gave you a rare old fright, didn't I? You looked about as sick as a dog!'

The old shepherd, George Abelard, looked at Philip reprovingly. 'You shouldn't do things like that, Master Philip. You ought to be ashamed of yourself.'

'It was only a joke,' Philip said. 'He shouldn't have let himself be taken in.'

And, seizing hold of Jim's arm, he was soon urging him to

leave Abelard and the flock to go ratting with the groom and the dogs.

After three weeks at Peele Jim was scarcely the same boy that Oakley had collared in the turnip field. The bruises and sores had vanished completely, leaving his skin a clear healthy pink, and his straight, fair, almost colourless hair, washed every day by Mrs Abelard, was now as smooth and fine as silk. He was also filling out; the pinched look had gone from his face and flesh was beginning to cover his bones. His eyes, too, these days, were a brighter blue and often twinkled with merriment.

'All thanks to you, Mrs Abelard, and the trouble you've taken with him,' Sutton said. 'But what are we going to do with him when Philip starts going to his lessons again?'

'You said you were going to make enquiries and see about finding that uncle of his.'

'What enquiries am I to make? Where should I start? You just tell me that! We neither know what the man is called, nor what he looks like, nor where he's from. Jim's accent is a mystery. It tells us just about nothing. And even if we found the man, would *you* hand the boy over to him, knowing what a brute he is and how Jim has suffered at his hands?'

'No, I would not,' Mrs Abelard said. 'The bruises he had when he came here – '

'Exactly so, Mrs Abelard, and therefore it seems to me that Jim had better stay with us and go with Philip to the vicarage for the parson to teach him to read and write. How would you like that, young man? Would it suit you, do you think?'

Jim gave a nod.

'He nods to everything, this boy, except when he shakes his head,' Sutton said. He turned to his son. 'What do you think of my idea, that we should keep Jim with us?'

'I thought we were going to, anyway.'

'Glad to have a brother, eh?'

'No, not a brother,' Philip said.

'What, then?' Sutton asked.

Philip gave a little shrug. 'Jim can be my servant,' he said.

Sutton, laughing, turned back to Jim.

'Did you hear that?'

'Yes, I did.'

'And do you agree to it?'

'No, I don't.' Jim's eyes were very blue and the jut of his chin as he looked up at Sutton showed that he had a will of his own. 'I want to work on the farm,' he said.

'Well, and so you shall, my boy. When you are old enough, that is. But first a little schooling, I think, to give you a good start in life. I'll see Parson Bannister in the morning on my way into town.'

So every day Jim went with Philip in the dog-cart to the vicarage at Lyall St Mary's where Mr Bannister, primed by Sutton, took his education in hand.

'What am I to teach the boy?' the vicar had asked, somewhat wearily.

'The three R's,' Sutton had said, 'and whatever else he wants to learn.'

Jim was very happy at Peele and his only anxiety was that his uncle might come back for him.

'Now why should he do that,' Mrs Abelard asked him, 'when you say he wanted to be rid of you?'

'He could change his mind, couldn't he?'

'But he doesn't know you're here with us. He'll think you're in the workhouse by now. And if by chance the brute did come here, why, he'd get my rolling-pin over his head!'

Jim was able to laugh at this; indeed he was laughing quite often now; and as the happy months went by, bringing a sense of security, his fears gradually died away until they became a thing of the past. And with the passing of his fears, he at last revealed his name.

'Jim Lundy?' Philip laughed. 'No wonder you kept it secret so long. It's almost as bad as Murgatroyd.'

'Oh no it isn't!'

'It is!'

'It's not!'

'And where did you come from?' Sutton asked. 'What part of the country were you raised?'

'I don't know. All over the place.'

'Don't you remember your parents, boy?'

'No, they died when I was small.'

'And then your uncle took charge of you?'

'No, it was my grannie at first. We lived in a place near the sea – my grannie called it Derry Coomb. Then my grannie got ill and died. Uncle Albert came for me – he was the drover. We moved about. He didn't like to stay in one place. We came up here from Salisbury Plain. Before that we were on the downs. And before that . . .' Jim spread his hands. 'Before that we were everywhere.'

'So! You're Jim Lundy from everywhere, or nowhere, whichever you please.'

Sutton eyed the boy searchingly, wondering if the story was true, but so far during his six months at Peele, Jim had never once told a lie, even to get himself out of trouble, and Sutton was inclined to believe him now.

'Anyway, true or not, it doesn't much matter, does it?' he said, speaking to the housekeeper afterwards. 'It's all worked out pretty well on the whole and Jim is adapting admirably. It's good for Philip to have another boy to play with and he seems to like Jim well enough, allowing for boyish squabbles, of course.'

'What young Master Philip likes is having someone to boss about and lead into mischief at every turn. *That's* what Master Philip likes.'

'Ah, well,' Sutton said, 'you're only young once, Mrs Abelard.'

Certainly the boys got into mischief, what with bringing hedgehogs into the house and putting a number of tiny elvers into Alice's chamber-pot; and certainly, more often than not, it was Jim who owned up to these pranks while Philip denied all knowledge of them. They got up to mischief on the farm, too, and once they wedged a sack full of sheep-raddle over the half-open door of a shed, so that when the door was opened wide the raddle fell on the person below. This happened to be Warren

Oakley and he, always lacking in humour, especially where boys were concerned, complained angrily to John Sutton.

'Dammit, man,' Sutton said, 'weren't you ever a boy yourself?' And when the bailiff continued to grumble, showing his skin still stained by the raddle, Sutton said pleasantly: 'Maybe you're feeling your age these days and think it's time you retired?'

Oakley was silenced by this covert threat, for Sutton paid better wages than any other farmer in the district, and Oakley, in his early sixties, had no wish to retire yet.

When he was not at the vicarage, having lessons with the vicar, Jim spent all his time on the farm, watching the work going on in the fields and, if allowed, joining in. But Philip's favourite activities were those of the young gentleman: shooting, fishing and riding to hounds. He soon became bored with talking to the 'yawnies' on the farm and would try to coax or challenge Jim into some more adventurous exploit. The two boys were much indulged and were given plenty of money to spend; they had the best rods and guns and two good ponies of their own to ride; and, for the most part, they enjoyed a great deal of freedom.

In winter Philip lived for the hunting. He could think and talk of nothing else. And one morning at the end of the season, when the last meet should have taken place, the boy, on being woken by Alice and told that there was a hard ground frost, burst into a storm of tears. Alice stood laughing at him, teasing him for being a cry-baby, and Philip, flying into a rage, seized the pitcher of hot water she had brought into his room and emptied most of it over her. His father threatened to thrash him for this but Alice, who was not much hurt, pleaded so gently on his behalf that he escaped with a telling-off.

Later that same day there was a partial thaw and Philip, still in a state of disappointment, persuaded the groom, Charlie Clements, to let him and Jim take their ponies out for an afternoon ride around the valley.

'All right, Master Philip, but no trotting or cantering, mind.

Just a gentle walk, that's all. The frost is only thawing on top, and the ground's still stone-hard down below.'

'I know that, I'm not a fool,' Philip said peevishly.

By an odd stroke of fate, however, as the two boys rode slowly through the beechwoods, a fox emerged from the undergrowth and moved off in front of them and Philip instinctively gave chase. Just as instinctively Jim went after him and when the fox broke from the wood, making across open pasture, the two boys followed at a trot that soon became a canter.

At the lower end of the pasture there was a deep dry ditch and the fox went down into this ditch, ran along it a little way, then leapt out at the other side and began crossing the ploughland beyond. Philip was highly excited by now and leapt his pony straight over the ditch. It was a very easy jump but the ploughland on the other side, lying as it did in the shade, was still iron-hard with frost, and the pony, jarring his forefeet on it, stumbled, checked, stumbled again, and finally fell onto his knees, with Philip sprawling over his neck. Jim, leaping the ditch behind him, was barely able to avoid a collision, and such was the check to his own pony that he was thrown right over its head. The pony then ran off but soon slowed down to a walk which, to Jim's great distress, showed him lame in the near foreleg. Philip's pony was lame in both legs and it was a sad, silent procession that made its way back to the stables.

So Philip got a thrashing after all and so did Jim, and as their offence this time had been a serious one, Sutton had little mercy on them.

'Lord, he fairly lammed into me!' Philip said, in great misery. 'And he said if Beau's legs are not better in a week I shall get another leathering then.'

'Yes, he said the same to me.'

The boys could not sit down all day and even walking was difficult; but worse than this, for Jim at least, was the terrible feeling of guilt and shame. His pony, Sandboy, was suffering and *he* had caused it, needlessly. Worse, too, than Sutton's anger was Charlie Clements's quiet distress and the patient, restrained, perplexed manner in which he reproached the two boys.

'I dunno how you could do such a thing, after what I said to you. Those two ponies, they're such trusting brutes – they'd go through hell and high water for you. And that's just what's happening now – they're going through hell, the pair of them, and all on account of your selfishness.'

'They will get better, though, won't they?' Jim said, in a voice he could only just control. 'They won't be in pain much longer, will they, now that we're looking after them?'

' "We?" ' Charlie said sardonically.

'Yes, I want to help,' Jim said.

'I reckon you've done enough,' Charlie said, but at the sight of Jim's face he relented. 'All right. You can help. So long as you do just what I say.'

'Much better leave it to Charlie,' said Philip. 'He's a marvel at doctoring horses, aren't you, Charlie, old man?'

Philip was never much troubled with guilt. He blamed his misfortunes on bad luck. If only there hadn't been a frost that day . . . Or if only that fox hadn't come along . . . Anyway, if he had done wrong, he had been thrashed, hadn't he, so surely that was the end of it?

'It doesn't help Beau and Sandboy,' Jim said.

'Neither does your long face,' said Philip.

When Jim was not in the stables, helping to change the coldwater bandages on Sandboy's sprained foot and Beau's sprained knees, he was out searching the hedgerows, picking the fresh, succulent greenstuff just beginning to grow there. Both ponies were fond of coltsfoot and cow parsley and with these, in a day or two, Jim was able to tempt them to eat. In a week they were much improved; in two weeks they were themselves again.

'Thank goodness for that!' Philip said. 'The stable's been like a morgue lately.'

For him the incident was over and the only question that troubled his mind was how long would it be before Beau could be ridden again. For Jim, however, it was different; what had happened to the two ponies still weighed heavily on him, and when, not long afterwards, Philip suggested some prank that had a flavour of mischief in it, Jim refused to take part.

'What's the matter with you,' Philip asked, 'acting so pi' all of a sudden?'

'I don't like getting into trouble.'

'You mean you don't like getting thrashed.'

'It's not only the thrashing itself. We did wrong, laming Sandboy and Beau like that, and we deserved every stroke we got. But I don't like doing wrong. It makes me feel bad inside. And I intend to make sure that I don't get into trouble again.'

Philip jeered at him over this.

'Jim's a goody-two-shoes these days,' he said to Mrs Abelard. 'He never wants to do anything in case it gets him into trouble. It's only because he got thrashed that time. It's made a coward out of him.'

'That's not cowardly. That's common sense. It's all very well for you, Master Philip, you're the master's own son. But Jim's only a poor boy who's got to make his way in the world. That means watching his p's and q's, and keeping on the right side of people, especially his elders and betters. So you just leave him be, Master Philip, and don't go calling him nasty names.'

'Oh, I might have guessed that you'd stick up for him!' Philip said. 'Housekeeper's pet, isn't he? But he'd better watch his p's and q's keeping on the right side of *me* as well, because I shall be master here one day and that's something he seems to forget!'

Jim was inclined to laugh at this.

'What will you do? Turn me out?'

'I could do if I wanted! I could get you turned out this very minute if I went to my father and asked him to do it. You wouldn't care for that, would you, going back to being a drover?'

'No. But there are worse things.'

'Such as what?' Philip asked.

'Well,' Jim said, deliberately, and although he was still amused at the turn the conversation had taken, his answer was made in all earnestness, 'I'd rather be a drover any day than stop in a place where I wasn't wanted.'

'There, Master Philip!' Mrs Abelard said. 'I hope you're satisfied with that, because I reckon we've had enough talk about turning people out of the house. And all of it blowing up like a storm just because Jim won't go out with you.'

'I never said I wouldn't go out with him, Abby. I said I wouldn't do anything that landed us in trouble again.'

'Shooting rabbits won't land us in trouble!' Philip said scornfully.

'Well, so long as it's only rabbits,' Jim said.

'It wouldn't be anything else, would it? Not now the breeding season's begun?'

With this assurance from Philip, Jim went willingly enough to shoot rabbits in the plantation just behind the old farm-house. But again they were dogged by the 'bad luck' that always seemed to put temptation in Philip's way and as they were returning home, each with a brace of rabbits in his satchel, they came upon a hen pheasant sitting on her nest in the undergrowth. For a moment the two boys stood looking at her and although they were only some twelve feet away, she continued to sit, quite motionless, her red eyes fixed in a bright, hard stare. Jim could sense that Philip, beside him, was itching to get a shot at her, and he moved to take hold of Philip's arm.

'No, you can't! You mustn't!' he said, speaking with quiet vehemence. 'Can't you see she's on her nest?'

Philip, with an excited laugh, pulled himself free of Jim's grasp and went on his way. As he went he stumbled, however, – on purpose, it seemed to Jim – and the noise frightened the pheasant into flight. She rose explosively, with a loud cry, and went whirring off between the trees. In the same instant Philip swung round, unbreaking his gun, which was already loaded, and bringing it swiftly to his shoulder. He was a very good shot and brought the pheasant down at once. There was a thump as it hit the ground; a flutter of feathers in the air; and Philip, with a satisfied grunt, went forward to pick up his prize.

But the pheasant, shot at such close range, was badly damaged. Philip held it up by the legs, turning it this way and that, his flushed face expressing triumph equally mixed with disgust. Then, as Jim came up, he said: 'Look at her! She's all shot to bits! I should've counted up to five.'

'What does it matter?' Jim said coldly. 'You couldn't have taken it home, anyway, or you would have got a leathering.'

'I know that! D'you think me a fool? I'd have sold it to Manders at the inn. He's paid me a florin for a pheasant before, but he won't look at a bird full of lead.'

'And just for the chance of a florin,' Jim said, 'you shot a bird sitting on her nest!'

'She wasn't sitting. She got up.'

'You put her up on purpose,' Jim said.

'So what if I did? It's no business of yours! And if you hadn't kept so close to me I should've taken more careful aim and got her without damaging her. As it is, she's no use at all. Food for magpies! That's all she is!'

They were near the edge of the wood and Philip, going to the fence, hurled the dead pheasant over into the pasture beyond. He wiped his bloodstained hand on his jacket and turned back towards the woodland path. Jim, in silence, followed him.

The incident did not end there, however, for the pheasant was picked up by one of the farm boys, Peter Gray, when he was sent to bring in the cows. Peter hid the bird inside his jacket, but the bailiff, noticing the bulge, asked to see what was causing it and, on discovering the pheasant, accused Peter of having shot it. The taking of game by the farm-hands was a serious matter at any time and almost certainly meant dismissal; but this offence, in the breeding season, so incensed John Sutton that he threatened to send for the parish constable with a view to bringing a charge. Peter Gray, very upset, protested that it was all a mistake and his story was convincing enough to give Sutton pause. He left Peter in his office and went in search of Philip and Jim.

'Have you been out shooting today?'

'Yes, father,' Philip said.

'Did you shoot a hen pheasant in the plantation or the pasture nearby?'

'No, father. Just rabbits, that's all. Abby will tell you. I gave them to her.'

Sutton now questioned Jim.

'Did *you* shoot a pheasant by any chance?'

'Jim wasn't there!' Philip said. 'He didn't go with me, did you, Jim?'

'I'd sooner Jim spoke for himself,' Sutton said, in forbidding tones, and his gaze remained fixed on Jim's face. 'Well, I am waiting for your answer, boy.'

'I *was* in the wood,' Jim said.

'And were you with Philip or were you not?'

'Well,' Jim said evasively.

'Peter Gray has just been found with a dead hen pheasant in his possession. I was going to send for the constable but Peter says he found the pheasant lying in the woodside pasture. Now, Jim, I ask you again – did you shoot a pheasant today?'

'No. I did not.'

'Did Philip shoot one?'

'Yes,' Jim said.

'What became of it?' Sutton asked.

'He threw it over into the pasture.'

'All right, Jim, you may go. Philip, come with me to the office. You can hear what I say to Peter Gray and afterwards, when he's gone back to work, you can bring me the cane.'

After this second thrashing, Philip came storming into the kitchen to vent his fury on Jim, who was talking to Mrs Abelard.

'Damned dirty, filthy sneak, telling tales on me like that! You got me six lashes! Hard ones too! But that's what you wanted, isn't it?'

'Don't blame me for what you got. If you'd spoken up in the first place instead of telling that stupid lie –'

'Oh, you never tell lies, of course! You never do any wrong at all!'

'Peter Gray could've lost his place on account of that pheasant of yours. He might even have gone to gaol. Some-

31

body had to speak up for him and if only you'd had a bit of sense – '

'That's not why you told on me! You did it to get me a thrashing, that's all! You've always been jealous of me from the start because I am my father's son and you're nothing but a little turd that somebody left on our doorstep!'

Philip went out again, slamming the door, and Mrs Abelard looked at Jim.

'Master Philip's a fine one to talk about your being jealous,' she said, 'when the boot is on the other foot.'

'Is it?' Jim said in surprise. 'But why should Philip be jealous of me? I haven't got anything he wants.'

'Just as well,' Mrs Abelard said, 'or he'd have it off you like a shot.'

'Why would he?'

'Because he's spoilt.'

'I don't think I *am* jealous of Philip,' Jim said, still considering the matter.

'Well, now, and what if you were? It wouldn't hardly be very surprising, seeing Master Philip's got so much and you're a poor boy with nothing at all.'

'Poor?' Jim said, surprised again. 'I wouldn't say I was poor, Abby. I'd say I was very lucky indeed.'

'Yes, so you are, Master Jim, and I'd be the first to tell you so, if you needed telling which you don't. After what you'd been used to, to come and live in this fine new house, with a good, kind man looking after you, giving you everything you want! Oh, yes, you are lucky indeed! But what sort of life will you have later on? That's the question that vexes me.'

'I'm going to work on the farm,' Jim said.

'Yes, I know,' Mrs Abelard said. 'But it seems all wrong to me, somehow, when you're being raised as you are now, and learning to live like a gentleman, that you should later be expected to work like a labourer on the land.'

'But I *want* to work on the land, Abby. I want it more badly than anything else. And I'm not a gentleman, as you know, nor shall I ever be, come what may.'

'No, Master Jim,' Mrs Abelard said. 'You're neither flesh

nor fowl nor good red herring and that's why I feel sorry for you. Still, you'll be all right, I daresay, for you've got a good headpiece on you and you know how to make the most of yourself. But you need to watch out for Master Philip, especially now you're both getting older, because he'll always do you down if he can. It's not that he's a wicked lad but he's got to come first in everything. So mind what I say and watch out for yourself and that way you won't ever come to no harm. Understand me, Master Jim?'

Jim nodded.

'I shall watch out for myself, Abby. You may be quite sure of that.'

Chapter Three

Mrs Abelard was not the only one to worry about Jim's future; the vicar, Mr Bannister, was also concerned; and one day in the summer of 1847 he mentioned the matter to John Sutton.

'Jim's future?' Sutton said. 'What do you mean?'

'Well, he's being brought up with your own son, and yet he is not your own son. May I ask – forgive me – but do you intend to make Jim equal with Philip later on?'

'Good God, no! Certainly not! Jim is going to work on the farm. Work is his portion, he knows that quite well. He'll make a good bailiff one day – better than Oakley, I suspect – and a not-too-distant day at that.'

'Ah, yes. Very suitable.'

'And yet you're still worried. Now why is that? Has he not been behaving himself?'

'Oh, yes. He behaves very well.'

'Does he work at his lessons?'

'Yes, indeed. In fact that is perhaps the problem. He is doing almost too well. Quite remarkable, really, for a boy of his beginnings. He was, as you know, almost completely illiterate when he first came to me, but now he not only reads and writes but has made such good progress with his Latin that he has actually caught up with Philip. Then, again, in mathematics – '

'Are you trying to tell me that Jim is a better scholar than Philip?'

'Well, no, not exactly. It's all a question of application – '

'Then Philip must be made to learn a little application, too, though you've left it rather late in the day to remedy that yourself, seeing that soon he will be going to school.' John

Sutton was somewhat nettled. He thought the vicar a feeble fellow. 'But you said you wanted to discuss Jim and I still haven't got to the bottom of what it is you're trying to say.'

'It's really quite simple,' the vicar said. 'Jim is getting an education better suited to a gentleman than the farm bailiff he is going to be and I think, if we continue with it, it may cause problems later on.'

'Make him discontented, you mean, and give him ideas above his station? Yes, well, you may be right.'

Feeble fellow he might be but, now he had come to the point at last, the vicar was talking good sense.

'What do you advise me to do?'

'I think, when Philip starts going to school, Jim should stop his lessons with me and start work on the farm straight away. After all, he's nearly thirteen, and most boys of his class would have been working long ago. I shall be sorry to lose such a good pupil but I think it's in his own best interests. He's got to find his proper level, and if we leave it too long, that may prove very hard for him.'

'Yes, you're right,' Sutton said. 'He's had a good grounding with you, anyway, and that's about what I had in mind when I sent him to you. I'm glad you mentioned the matter to me. I shall do exactly as you say.'

In the second week in September, therefore, when Philip went off to Surpingham, Jim began work on the farm.

'The boy is to learn everything,' Sutton said to Oakley, the bailiff. 'He'll be treated like any other farm boy and do exactly the same work. Is that understood?'

'Yes, if he hasn't been spoilt for it,' Oakley muttered under his breath; and to Jim, as he led him away, he said, 'Bit of a come-down for you, isn't it, doing some real work for a change?'

But Jim himself had no such feelings. The farm was where he wanted to be. He had never had any doubts about that, and if his lessons with the vicar had absorbed him, his lessons in farmyard and cowshed and field absorbed him even more completely. He was strong, healthy, and energetic, and exulted in his ability to tackle any job on the farm. The work, far from degrading him, brought him satisfaction and joy. He liked nothing better than to take off his coat and roll up his sleeves and 'get pitched in', as old Abelard said. And Philip, home for the holidays, watching Jim heaving and sweating, pitching sheaves to the threshing machine, or loading dung into a cart, would laugh at the vigour and cheerfulness with which he toiled.

'You never seem to mind getting yourself in a muck sweat. I suppose that's the peasant in you.'

'Arr, if thee zay zo, zir,' Jim said with a grin, and tugged at the peak of his corduroy cap.

John Sutton's plan was that Jim should spend two years working with the cowman, two with the carters, and two with the shepherd, George Abelard. This suited Jim very well; he wanted to know everything that cowman and carter could teach him; but his greatest friend on the farm had always been George Abelard and any spare moment he had was spent helping with the flock.

Because of his special interest in sheep he was always allowed 'time off' in the spring so that he could help with the lambing and this was perhaps the happiest of all the year's happy seasons. He would spend a good many days at a stretch up in the lambing field under the hill and would sleep at night with the old shepherd in his hut on wheels, waking to the slightest sound in the pens as quickly as Abelard did himself. Jim had a sort of instinct for sheep; an understanding of their needs; a sympathy with them so acute that by the time he was fourteen he already had the shepherd's gift for sensing in advance that a certain ewe would need help in lambing.

'You're the best helper I ever had,' Abelard said to him once, and this was high praise indeed, for the old shepherd was hard to please.

Jim was not paid with the other farm employees because he already received an allowance, just as Philip did, and this custom was kept up even though he now worked on the farm.

36

Jim's allowance was ten shillings and to him it always seemed a fortune, for even grown men on the farm received no more than this, and they had families to feed and clothe, whereas Jim's ten shillings was his to spend just as he pleased.

In fact he spent very little and in this he was different from Philip who, although he received a whole guinea, was always 'skint' by Wednesday or Thursday and badly in debt by Saturday night. Often Philip would ask Jim to lend him a shilling or two and in the early days Jim would oblige. But there came a time later on when Philip, home for the holidays, borrowed half-a-crown from Jim and returned to school without paying it back. So the next time he was at home and asked Jim for a loan he met with a forthright refusal.

'Lord, you are a mean old stick! You must have stacks of tin put away, always saving the way you do. What are you going to do with it?'

'You'll see one of these days.'

'Do you have to be so mysterious? Can't you answer a chap straight out?'

'All right, I'll tell you,' Jim said. 'I intend to buy some sheep.'

'What on earth for?' Philip asked.

'For one thing, I happen to like them,' Jim said. 'For another, they'll make a good investment.'

'Well, you'll have to ask my father's permission before you start keeping sheep of your own, since you'll be raising them here on our land.'

'Yes, of course, I intend to,' Jim said.

John Sutton gave his permission without any hesitation and at the autumn sheep fair that year Jim bought twenty Cotswold shearling ewes – theaves as old Abelard called them – and a Cotswold ram to go with them. The Peele flock consisted of Downs and Leicesters and Jim chose to keep a different breed so that his twenty-one sheep could be picked out easily from the rest.

His 'investment' cost him thirty-eight pounds, but he had only to walk out into the pasture and see his sheep grazing there, their thick curly fleeces a rich pale gold in the autumn

37

sunlight, to feel that they were worth every penny even of this huge sum. The pride he took in them was immense. There were no sheep like them in the whole world. And because of them he was much chaffed by the men and boys on the farm.

'Here comes the flockmaster,' they would say, and once the head carter, Joe Greening, pinned a bunch of 'daglocks' in Jim's cap, saying, 'There, now you look the part to a tee.'

Jim's flock lambed in April, giving him twenty-six lambs, and of these he lost only two. One of the original ewes proved barren and she was sold off with the twenty-four lambs early in August. Together with the sale of the wool, Jim's profit that year amounted to some forty pounds and the Suttons, who were with him at the sale, watched in amusement as he stowed his money away in a small washleather bag.

'Ah, Jim will end up richer than any of us, you mark my words,' John Sutton said with a laugh. And Philip, with a look of disdain, replied, 'He'll end up a miser if you ask me.'

At the sheep fair in October Jim, again with Sutton's permission, bought twenty-one ewes, so that he now had forty in all. Thus, in the following spring, his flock yielded fifty-three lambs, fifty of which he reared successfully, and that year his total profits amounted to eighty-eight pounds. Once again he planned to buy a new draft of ewes but this time John Sutton was less ready with his permission.

'How many were you thinking of buying?'

'Another twenty.'

'H'm,' Sutton said, doubtfully. 'Well, I think myself it would be better if you were to buy just ten, and keep your flock to a round fifty. That's plenty big enough for you to manage, what with your proper work as well, and we don't want the land getting sheep-sick, do we, eh?'

'No, sir,' Jim said.

But he was puzzled by Sutton's edict, for the main flock at Peele had been reduced in recent years and there was no risk whatever that the two hundred sheep now kept would render the land sheep-sick.

'Why does Mr Sutton want me to keep my flock down to fifty?' he asked old Abelard. 'The farm doesn't carry nearly so many sheep as it used to, so why should he say that?'

Old Abelard gave a grunt.

'Mr Sutton's the master here and the master don't have to have any reasons for what he says to us underlings. We've got to be kept in our place, you see, and it seems that goes the same for you as it does for all the rest of us, even though you're a special case and have been brought up with the master's son.'

Jim made a face. He was somewhat cast down.

'It seems I've been overstepping the mark. Getting above myself, as they say. Had I better give up my flock altogether, d'you think? After all, I do graze them on Peele land.'

Old Abelard shook his head. His hand rested briefly on Jim's arm.

'You keep your flock,' he said quietly. 'Keep 'em so long as you're allowed. That's your investment, isn't it? Your stake in the future, as you might say. It gives you a bit of independence and no doubt that goes against the grain in certain quarters, if you follow me, but don't you worry too much about that. Your little flock isn't doing no harm. As for grazing Peele land, why, they manure it at the same time, don't they? And many a flock gets its keep free for doing that.'

So Jim kept his little flock and tended them with earnest care, culling those ewes that were sickly or barren and replacing them with vigorous theaves, but always, conscientiously, keeping their number to the round fifty that John Sutton had stipulated. And every year his profits were such that he added upwards of eighty-five pounds to his savings in one of the Missenham banks.

Philip was always scornfully amused at Jim's interest in sheep. He did not care for them at all. There were 'poor man's stock', he said, and out of place now on a farm like Peele.

'If I had my way, I'd get rid of them all. We only keep them for tradition's sake. We no longer need the Golden Hoof, not with modern farming methods, and God knows there's no real money in them.'

39

Old Abelard disagreed. 'You're wrong there, Master Philip. There's money in sheep, sure enough, only it's silver, you see, not gold. But silver mounts up in time, you know, if only you've got the patience to let it.'

Philip, with a smile, looked at Jim.

'And is the silver mounting up for you?'

'I'm not complaining,' Jim said.

'How much have you got in the bank so far?'

'I don't see why I should tell you that.'

'God! You are a secretive beggar! I don't know why I talk to you. And what are you going to do with it – all this money you're putting away?'

'I hope one day, if all goes well, to rent a few acres of land of my own.'

'A smallholding?'

'Yes, that's right.'

'But you're going to be our bailiff here and take over from Oakley when he gets old.'

'I can easily do both. Many a bailiff does that.'

'Small farms are a thing of the past. They're uneconomic. They're suicide. You've only got to look at Godsakes, going to ruin over there. That's a hundred and ten acres and yet just look at the state it's in. Fields overgrown with brambles and thorns! Stock reduced to nothing at all. House and buildings falling down!'

'That's nothing to do with the size of the farm. It's a good-sized farm, taken all round, what with the hill pastures and common rights on the meadows and all. It's just that Riddler has had bad luck and isn't very good at managing things.'

'Bad luck my eye! The damned fool bit off more than he could chew when he decided to buy that place. A man's got no business buying land when he hasn't even got the money to pay for it let alone do right by it!'

'No, well, you may be right, but there's more to it than that, isn't there?' The story behind Riddler's misfortunes was as well known to Jim as it was to Philip himself, for it was often discussed at Peele and John Sutton made no bones about the part he had played in it. 'It's not entirely Riddler's fault, is it, that he ran into trouble over money when he first bought his farm?'

'He blames my father. We all know that. And to judge by the way you're talking now, it seems as though you take Riddler's side.'

'I don't know about taking sides, but I'm sorry for Riddler, I must admit.'

'Sorry for him!' Philip exclaimed. 'After what he's done to that farm, letting it go to rack and ruin, an eyesore and a damned disgrace? Why, my father says it'll take five years to put that land in order again, when we do get hold of it. Hanging on by the skin of his teeth, year in, year out, the way he does! He only stays there to spite us and stop us getting our hands on it. And yet you say you feel sorry for him!'

Philip turned and marched off and old Abelard said to Jim:

'It doesn't do to stick up for Morris Riddler. Not with the master or his son. The master's been waiting a long time to get his hands on that farm and it's a sore subject with him that he hasn't managed it so far.'

'I suppose he'll have to give up in the end? Riddler, I mean.'

'It's only fair amazing to me that he's hung on as long as he has, but that's how it is in farming, you see. It can take a man twenty years to go to ruin good and proper. And I reckon it's a terrible thing, to see land go back like that, and the people on it brought so low that they're scarcely nothing better than beggars. It's Riddler's wife and young daughter I feel most sorry for, stuck over there, working so hard, scarcely ever leaving the place from one year's end to the next. If Riddler's got any feeling for them he should sell up and get out and give them the chance of a decent life.'

'Yes, I suppose he should,' Jim said. 'But if I were Riddler and had my own farm I reckon I'd feel the same as he does. I'd stick it out to the very end and fight for it to the last breath.'

'Well, that's what he's doing, sure enough,' Abelard said, with a shake of his head.

It happened not long after this that Jim had a meeting with

Morris Riddler. It was a day in early August and he had gone with the other Peele men to begin cutting a field of corn on that part of the farm that had once been Granger's and which lay on the same side of the valley as Godsakes. The men were at work with their scythes, cutting a broad path round the field, to make way for the reaping machine, when the warm west wind, blowing down from Godsakes, brought with it a scent of hay so exceedingly sweet and strong that the men stopped work and sniffed the air.

'Riddler's got a hot stack,' said Joe Greening, and turned to look up at Godsakes, rising in a series of grey-green fields beyond the boundary of Granger's. 'There it is. At the top there, look.' And he pointed to an ungainly haystack standing in a deserted field immediately under Hogden Hill. 'Whew!' he said, sniffing again. 'That'll go up in flames directly if something isn't done about it.'

'Going to tell him about it, are you?' Arthur Slatter asked slyly, for the Peele men, these nine years past, had kept clear of Morris Riddler for fear of offending their employer.

'Somebody ought to,' Greening said.

And Jim, putting away his scythe, volunteered.

Riddler had been milking his cows and was letting them out into the pasture when Jim came up the adjoining field and spoke to him over the farmyard wall.

'You've got a hot stack,' he said, and pointed in its general direction. 'In the field with a hut in it, just under the hill. It'll go up in flames, Joe Greening says, if you don't do something about it soon.'

'Damn and blast!' Riddler said. 'If it isn't one damned thing it's another!' He closed the gate behind the last cow and came across the yard to the wall. 'Did Joe Greening send you to me?'

'He said somebody ought to come.'

'That was good of him. Good of you, too. Your master would never have done that. *He'd* have stood and watched it burn,' Riddler was eyeing Jim curiously. 'You're Jim Lundy, aren't you?' he said. 'The boy Sutton found in his barn that time? I've seen you about these many years, but never close to like this before.' Resting his folded arms on the wall, he looked

42

across the valley at Peele and gave a slight lift of his grey stubbled chin. 'I see the lot of you, over there, coming and going about the place. You look like a lot of puppets from here and no doubt we look the same to you.'

'Yes,' Jim said, and the thought made him smile.

He was just as curious about Riddler, seeing him close for the first time, as Riddler was about him; but, being a boy, barely seventeen, he was rather less open about it and only when the man's queer, crooked face was averted did he steal a few quick glances at him. And after these quick glances he found himself wondering how it was that Morris Riddler, who was not really a big man, should nevertheless give an impression of bull-like solidity and strength.

'Does John Sutton treat you all right?'

'Yes. He treats me very well.'

'Expects you to work, though, doesn't he?'

'Everyone has to work,' Jim said.

'He used to treat *me* pretty well, too, until it suited him not to. But no doubt you know that old tale . . . John Sutton's side of it, anyway.' Riddler's gaze came back to Jim's face. 'Is he still waiting to buy me out?' he asked with harsh jocularity. 'Still waiting like a carrion crow to have my carcass, is he, eh?'

'I must get back to work,' Jim said. He turned away.

'Hang on a minute. I'll walk down with you and look at that stack.'

Riddler, with awkward agility, climbed over the farmyard wall and dropped down beside Jim. Together they walked down the sloping fields, all of which, in one way or another, were in an advanced state of neglect. In one a dozen sheep were grazing and Jim, who had passed them on the way up, now carefully looked away, for the sheep had not yet been shorn, although it was August, and their wool hung from them in tatters, scratched off on the thorn bushes that grew dotted about the field.

'All a bit different from Peele, eh?' Riddler said, as they walked along. 'Those few sheep of mine, now. Different from Sutton's Leicesters, eh? Different from your little flock of Cotswold Lions, aren't they, eh?'

43

Jim, at a loss, said nothing, and Riddler, perceiving his surprise, laughed deep down in his throat.

'I see what goes on over there, you know, just as you see what goes on over here. And I hear most of the gossip, too, especially on market days. Well, this is where we part. Did I say thanks about the stack? Yes, well, I'm obliged to you – if any man can be obliged when somebody brings him bad news!'

He went off with a wave of his hand and Jim went back to join the mowers in the cornfield.

'What did he say?' Joe Greening asked.

'He said he was obliged to us.'

'And what are things like up there, when you see the place close to?'

'Pretty bad,' Jim said, 'but Riddler seems cheerful enough.'

'Yes, well, from what I hear, there's a reason for that,' Greening said. 'His wife's expecting a little un. But if Morris Riddler is pleased about it, I doubt very much if his wife feels the same. Not at her time of life, poor soul, and with only middling health at that.'

Chapter Four

It was not the first hot stack Riddler had had at Godsakes, and probably wouldn't be the last, for the two men he employed would sooner do a job badly than well. Whenever he grumbled at them they always made the same reply.

'If you only pay us six shillings a week, master, you only get six shillings' worth of work.'

'I'd think myself lucky,' Riddler would snarl, 'if only you did *three* shillings' worth!'

The stack had to be opened out. He sent Smith and Lovell to do it at once.

'And don't build it up again until I damn well tell you to!'

'You told us to build it in the first place,' said Smith, 'and I knew all along that hay wasn't fit.'

'Then why the hell didn't you say so?' Riddler asked angrily.

Lovell and Smith merely walked away, 'trying to see how slow they could go', as Riddler often said of them, and he turned back into the yard, knowing that the job of opening the stack would probably take them all day. 'They'll see to that, sure enough!' he said, muttering under his breath.

His daughter, Kirren, came out of the house with a tub full of washing to hang on the line.

'How's your mother?'

'Just the same.'

'Still in bed, is she?'

'Yes, she's asleep.'

'H'mm,' he said absently, and stood for a while staring into space.

The dairymaid, Florrie Dixon, came out of the dairy with

two empty pails, filled them with water from the trough at the pump, and carried them back again, slop and splash. Riddler went across to the open cartshed and began rummaging about among a collection of old tools that stood in a corner. But all the time he was watching Kirren hanging up the clothes and when she had finished and gone indoors he left the cartshed, empty-handed, and went quietly into the dairy, pushing the door to behind him but not quite closing it.

After a while Kirren emerged from the house again with another tub full of washing. She set it down on the cobbles and began hanging the clothes on the line. Soon, however, she stopped and listened, hearing sounds in the dairy: her father's voice, quiet for once; the rattle of a pail; a muffled laugh. She went across to the dairy door and pushed it open and at the sound of its creaking hinge her father and the dairymaid sprang apart, he to look under the bench, as though searching for something there, she to take up a pan of cream and set it in place over the cooler.

Kirren, without saying a word, returned to her task. Her father came out of the dairy, went into the cartshed again, and this time came out carrying a hoe. For a moment he stood uncertainly, watching Kirren as she hung up the clothes, but her young face was closed against him and he went off with the hoe on his shoulder, swearing softly to himself.

At midday he returned for his dinner and while he was eating he spoke to Kirren about the incident in the dairy.

'You haven't told your mother, I hope, about seeing me with Florrie Dixon?'

Kirren, in silence, flashed him a glance.

'No, well, better not,' he said. 'She might go and get the wrong idea.'

'I've no intention of telling her. She's got quite enough to bear as it is.'

'Yes. You're right. She has, that's a fact.' He put a piece of bread into his mouth and chewed it noisily, clicking his jaws. 'That girl, Florrie! She's full of sauce. She asks for trouble, the way she goes on. But what you saw . . . it was only a lark . . . and it won't ever happen again, not after today, be sure of that.'

46

'No, it won't, because Florrie is gone.'

'Gone?'

'Yes. I paid her off. She won't be coming here any more.'

'You had no right to do such a thing! How d'you think you're going to manage, doing all the dairywork, and no Florrie to give you a hand? Your mother can't do it. Not just now. And she's going to have her hands pretty full –'

'I shall manage perfectly well. In fact I'd sooner work by myself than have Florrie Dixon about the place. I never did care much for her.'

'Ah, now we come to it, don't we?' he said. 'You only got rid of the girl because you don't care for her!'

'You know why I got rid of her,' Kirren said, quietly, and under her dark, critical gaze Riddler was forced to look away.

'Well, if you think you can manage all right . . . It's a lot to do, for a girl of fifteen.'

'I can manage. I shall see that I do.'

He had finished his meal and now he rose.

'I'm going up to see your mother and have a bit of a chat with her.'

'How are you feeling now, Agnes? Feeling a bit better, are you?'

'Yes, Morris. Not too bad.'

'Then why aren't you up and about, instead of lying in bed like this? Such a beautiful hot summer day it is, and you always did say you liked it hot.'

'I don't seem to have the strength. I come over giddy when I get up. All I want to do is sleep.'

'There's more than three months to go yet,' Riddler said. 'And it's not as though it's your first, neither. You were all right with the other two. You had no trouble with them at all.'

'Didn't I?'

'Of course you didn't.'

'That was a long time ago, Morris, and I've lost three babies since then. I'm older, too.'

'Yes, but not so old as all that. You're forty-five, I don't call that old. If it was, you wouldn't be like you are, now, would you?'

'Oh, I'm young enough to be having a child,' Agnes said, wearily, 'and old enough to be dreading it.'

'Don't say that, Agnes, don't say that. It'll be all right, you mark my words. Now, what about drinking up your milk? It came from old Daisy – I milked her myself – and it's got a drop of something in it that didn't come from any cow! You drink it up. It'll do you good.'

Riddler, helping his wife to sit up, held the glass for her to drink. Then, having set the glass aside, he helped to make her comfortable, plumping the pillows up behind her and straightening the coverlet on the bed. He picked up the glass and stood looking at her.

'There, that'll soon buck you up,' he said. 'It'll put some colour into your cheeks and make you more like yourself again.' And after a pause he said huskily: 'It's lonely downstairs without you, old girl. I'll be glad when you're up and about again. I miss you, Agnes, and that's a fact.'

Riddler could not believe that his wife was ill, right up to the very last, and when she died he was drunk for three days. Hopelessly drunk, in a blind stupor, so that Kirren had to do everything.

On the morning of the funeral she went into the scullery, where her father lay on his back on the floor, and emptied a jug of cold water over him. Then she went back into the kitchen and a few minutes later he lumbered in after her and sat, groaning, in a chair at the table. Kirren put his breakfast in front of him, but he turned away from it, grey-faced and sick.

'Do you expect me to eat that when I've got to go down to Marychurch and see my wife put into the grave?'

'Eat it or not, as you please.'

'First Eddy. Now her. And the parson will talk some cant about God! What sort of God is it that takes away as good a wife as any man ever had?'

'It isn't God you should blame – it's yourself.'

'What do you mean?'

'You know what I mean.'

Riddler put his head in his hands but after a while he looked up again. 'We were hoping for a son.'

'*You* were hoping for a son.'

'We loved each other, your mother and me.'

'You may call it love if you like. I do not.'

'You're only a girl, you don't understand. You will do in time, when you've grown up a bit, especially when you're married yourself. You'll understand things better then . . . what a man feels for his wife. There's more to it than you think, and when he finds himself alone . . . Well, you don't understand, that's all. You've no idea what it's like.'

Suddenly Kirren turned on him.

'You seem to think you're the only one that's got any feelings!' she said. 'It was the same when Eddy died! He was mother's son as well as yours but you never gave her a single thought! It was what *you* felt! What *you* couldn't bear! And now we have it all over again! But how do you think *I* feel now that my poor mother is dead and all I've got left in the world is *you*?'

'It seems to me very hard that you should hold it against me for still being alive,' he said.

'I don't see why it should be so hard! You've held it against *me* all these years, because I'm alive and Eddy is not!'

'That's not true. That's rubbish, that is.'

'I heard you say it, out there in the yard. "Why did it have to be the boy that died?" That's what you said. I heard it myself.'

Riddler, sitting slumped in his chair, made a small, helpless gesture with his hands.

'Times like that, people say these things . . . But I didn't mean it, you must know that.'

'How should I know? I'm only a girl! I'm no use to you compared with a boy. You hoped all these years for another son and you killed my poor mother trying to get one. That's all I know.'

'I never said you were no use to me. When did I ever say such a thing? Girls've got their place in the world just exactly the same as boys. They become women, all in good time, and us men need them, there's no doubt of that. Where should I be if I hadn't got you? You're all I've got left to me now, Kirrie. You and the farm – that's all I've got left.'

Clumsily, he put out a hand, taking her arm and squeezing it.

'You're a good-sorted girl, I'll swear to that, and a better daughter than I deserve. There's only the two of us left now and we've both got to make the best of things. I should be lost without you, Kirrie, and I don't mind admitting it.'

Kirren's glance was sardonic. Firmly, she withdrew her arm. But her anger was gone. She spoke quietly now.

'Eat your breakfast. It's getting cold.'

Kirren had always been old for her years and at fifteen she was almost a woman: tall and slender, yet well-developed, with strong, supple arms and strong wrists, toughened by the work of the dairy: the turning of the heavy butter-churn and the long hours spent at the cheese-tub.

'You're growing into a good strong girl,' Riddler said to her once. 'You're as strong as a man in some respects and you've got a sort of knack, somehow, for doing things quick and sure.'

'It's just as well,' Kirren said, 'or I'd never get through the day's work at all.'

'You shouldn't have got rid of Florrie Dixon. I said you'd find the work too much.'

'Well, we're not having Florrie back, if that's what you are hinting at.'

'I can't see what harm there would be in it.'

'Well, you must decide between Florrie and me, because if you bring her here again, I shall leave home and never come back.'

'Hah! And where d'you think you'd go?'

'I should go into service on some other farm.'

Riddler muttered and grumbled and swore but, knowing

50

that this daughter of his always meant what she said, he had perforce to give in to her and go without the dubious comfort that Florrie Dixon would have given him. For although he might grumble at Kirren, he depended on her in too many ways to run the risk of losing her. Nobody else would work so hard, or manage the house so thriftily, and anyway, as he often said, she was all the kin he had left in the world and he looked forward to the time when she would marry and produce children, who would grow up to work on the farm and take over when he died.

Marriage, however, was a subject that filled Kirren with angry disgust.

'After seeing the life my mother had? One stillborn child after another? All the heartbreak, all the pain! And then to die at the end of it, aged forty-five, worn down to the very bone! Oh, no! That is not for me!'

'You don't know what you're talking about. You're still too young to understand. But somehow I can't see you ending up as an old maid.'

'You *will* see it, though, if you live long enough.'

And the next few years, far from changing her attitude, only seemed to harden it.

Kirren took after her mother in looks but was rather darker than Agnes had been, with hair so brown it was almost black, and skin as dusky as a gipsy's, especially in the summertime when she worked in the fields without a hat. At sixteen, she was growing attractive. At seventeen she was comely indeed. At least she would have been, Riddler thought, if only she were a little less sullen; a little less given to looking at you as though you were something the cat had brought in. Certainly the higgler, Billy Hayzell, who called at the farm once a week to buy Kirren's eggs and butter and cheese, found her attractive enough and was obviously very smitten with her.

Billy was rather a smug young man in his early twenties, deaf in one ear, and he used this as an excuse for coming right up to Kirren and putting his face close to hers.

'I can't properly hear you unless I can see your lips,' he

would say, but while standing so close to her he would try to steal an arm round her waist and once, catching her unawares, he succeeded in touching her cheek with a moist, warm, thick-lipped kiss.

Kirren, twisting away from him, let him have the full force of her wrath.

'If you ever try to do that again I'll fetch you such a mighty clout that you'll end up deaf in both your ears!' she said in a voice that rang round the yard.

Billy, calling at outlying farms, was apt to cheat his women customers, paying them prices well below those that their produce would have fetched in the market, knowing only too well that they could not get there easily themselves. Once when Kirren was grumbling to her father about the price Billy paid for her cheese he said he had little patience with her because it was all her own fault.

'If you weren't so hoity-toity with him, you could get good prices enough, I daresay. He's smitten with you, you know that full well. And if only you played your cards right, you could have him eating out of your hand.'

'You mean I should let him maul me about and fumble at me with his hot sticky hands? No, thank you! I'm not having that!'

'No, you'd sooner lose us the farm!' Riddler said with great bitterness. 'God knows we've come desperate close to it for want of some ready cash sometimes.'

'Don't you dare say that to me!' Kirren exclaimed, equally bitter. 'If we are in danger of losing the farm, it's you that's to blame for it, not me! *You* with your drinking on market days and all your foolish goings on!'

'You call that drinking?' Riddler said. 'Just a few glasses of ale once a week? You should see the way some of the chaps there drink! The spirits and suchlike they put away – '

'I don't want to see your chaps! One drunkard is more than enough for me!'

'You're not speaking fair, Kirrie, because I haven't been drunk since you know when. A glass or two, that's all I have, after doing business, perhaps.' Then, eyeing her critically and giving a shake of his head, he said: 'You'll never get a husband, the way you go on. You've no idea how to treat a man, Billy Hayzell or any other.'

'A husband is the last thing I want.'

'Hah, you don't know what you're missing, girl.'

'I know enough about it to make sure I stay as I am.'

'And who's going to take over the farm when I die, if you don't give me a grandson?'

'The farm, in all probability, will have gone under the auctioneer's hammer long before then,' Kirren said, 'and we may as well face up to that fact.'

Riddler, swearing, went off to the fields, and Kirren, studying her account book, tried to work out what profit, if any, she had made from the sale of her produce that day. The conclusion she came to so angered her that when Billy Hayzell called again, she told him in no uncertain terms that she would not deal with him any more, and she sent him away empty-handed.

Thereafter, to her father's disgust, she went in to the market herself, walking the three miles there and back, her two baskets heavy with produce on the journey in, and rather less heavy with provisions on the journey back.

'You must want seeing to,' Riddler said, 'traipsing all that way every week instead of dealing with Billy Hayzell at your own back door.'

'I make nearly half as much again on my produce as I did when I sold it to him. And I pay less for my groceries than when he used to get them for me.'

'Yes, and you're gone very nearly the whole day, when you are badly needed here.'

'Going in to Missenham is the one and only break I get. The one and only day in the week when I see a few fresh faces instead of just yours and Lovell's and Smith's. It's also the one and only day when I don't get shouted at all day long.'

'Yes, well,' Riddler said, suddenly growing rather reflective. 'I suppose it is pretty dull for you, stuck out here, off the beaten track, never meeting anyone much. I reckon you're doing the right thing, getting out and about a bit, going in to the market every week. You meet a good many people there. All sorts of people. Friendly, too.'

Kirren, knowing her father so well, saw the track his thoughts were taking.

'You mean I might find a husband there?'

'Well, you've got to look somewhere, haven't you?' Riddler said, cheerfully.

Chapter Five

In the autumn of 1855, under persuasion from John Sutton, Warren Oakley at last retired and Jim took over his duties as bailiff. The old man was given a pension and allowed to stay in the bailiff's house 'until such time,' Sutton said, 'as Jim should think of marrying and want to live in it himself.'

Jim now earned eighteen shillings a week which, for a young man of twenty-one, was riches indeed.

'You are well worth it,' Sutton said. 'I believe in paying good money to good men.'

Jim was certainly conscientious. Nothing escaped his watchful eye. And in spite of his extreme youth the men on the farm respected him, knowing that whatever job they were doing, he could do it as well as they. But he rarely took his coat off now; it was not expected of him; for the post of bailiff, on a farm such as Peele, carried with it a certain importance; even a certain amount of prestige. He wore a good suit of Cotswold tweed and rode a smart dapple grey horse. He was not expected to sweat now but to organize the work of the farm and see that it was carried out. He took pleasure and pride in his position and he was always acutely aware that, for a boy of such poor beginnings, he had really done very well for himself.

There was plenty of variety in his work and in winter, when there were guests in the house, most of whom came for the shooting, it was his job to make sure that the party got a good day's sport. These guests were all farmers from neighbouring counties; many of them were landowners; and among them were some of the foremost agriculturists of the day, whom John Sutton had got to know through the farming clubs. One of these was Sir Frederick Alton whose estate in Berkshire was said to be the most progressive in England. He was a friendly, affable man who got on well with everyone, whether high or low.

'Remarkable young chap, your bailiff,' he said to Philip Sutton one day. 'Not much he doesn't know about farming, even the latest developments. But he seems pretty well-informed all round and even quoted the Georgics to me this morning. How is it that a farm bailiff is so well-spoken and so well-read?'

'That is my father's doing,' Philip said. 'Jim Lundy was a foundling, left in one of our barns years ago, and my father took him into the house. He and I were brought up together, and my father paid for him to be educated by the local parson, along with me.'

'Yes, I see. That explains a good deal. He's certainly an intelligent young man. I quite thought he must be one of your own family.'

'Oh, no, sir. Indeed not. No relation whatsoever.'

'I thought of inviting him down to Langley, perhaps next year, when you come yourself. But then I had second thoughts and wondered if he could be spared from the farm?'

'To be honest, sir, I don't think he can. We do rather rely on him to keep things running smoothly here.'

'Yes, of course,' Sir Frederick said. 'Just as well I asked you first.'

Those of the Peele visitors who came every year were disgusted to see Godsakes growing more and more run-down, and becoming a terrible eyesore on the other side of the valley.

'There ought to be a law to stop men from occupying good land and letting it go to ruin like that.'

'Just what I feel myself,' Sutton said. 'But I don't think he'll last much longer now, for he owes money all over the place, and no one will give him credit any more. In fact, when you look across at that place, it's a wonder how he survives at all.'

'Then you think your patience will soon be rewarded?'

'I hope so, indeed,' Sutton said, with a smile. 'God knows I've waited long enough.'

Sometimes the Suttons, father and son, went on return visits to these friends, hunting with famous packs, and shooting over great estates of three thousand acres or more. At other times Philip went alone and often in the summer and autumn, when the agricultural shows were held, he had so many invitations that he would be absent for months at a time. John Sutton was not best pleased at this and once he took Philip to task about it.

'I don't want to spoil your fun, my boy, but I think it's time you settled down and found yourself a wife,' he said. 'This house has been without a mistress for more years than I care to remember and it's time you did something about it instead of gadding about all over the country, here, there, and everywhere.'

'You seem to forget,' Philip said, 'that there are three pretty girls at Langley.'

'Ah,' Sutton said, much mollified. 'So that's how the wind blows, is it, eh? And which of the trio do you favour or is it too soon to ask?'

'The youngest, Caroline,' Philip said, 'and when I go on my next visit there, I intend to propose to her.'

'Splendid! Splendid!' Sutton said. 'I couldn't have chosen better myself!'

This conversation took place early in 1858: a year that promised well, Sutton thought; a year that should see Godsakes Farm come into his possession at last; and if before the end of it, Philip should bring home a wife, well, he would ask for nothing more.

'I'm not getting any younger, you know. I'll be fifty-six in a month or so. And I'd like to see you produce an heir in time for me to get to know him.'

'I'll see what I can do,' Philip said.

It was in the spring of that same year that Jim met and fell in love with Jane Reynolds. Her father, who owned a glass manufactory in Birmingham, had recently rented Hide House Farm, near Abbot's Lyall, and John Sutton, as a good neighbour should, had soon called there, taking Jim with him.

57

Alec Reynolds had rented Hide House so that he and his wife and daughter should have all the benefits of living in the country; and the farm, of about a hundred acres, was to be his hobby. He confessed he knew nothing of farming as yet and Sutton immediately suggested that Jim should help and advise him.

'Jim will soon tell you what to do to get the best out of your land. You can't do better than listen to him.'

'That's uncommonly good of you.'

'Not at all,' Sutton said.

And that was how Jim, in the month of April, came to spend so much of his time at Hide House Farm and in doing so met Jane Reynolds. He was now twenty-four; Jane was eighteen; and all through the spring and early summer their friendship grew and blossomed, with Jane's easy-going parents looking on indulgently, and, so it seemed, with approval.

'Jim is such a nice young man and just the friend Jane needs, coming to a new district like this, where we hardly know anyone,' Mrs Reynolds said to John Sutton. And Alec Reynolds, on learning something of Jim's background, said to his wife: 'Well, the boy is not exactly a catch, having no family of his own, but he's certainly made the best of himself, with Sutton's help, and I daresay if he were to marry, Sutton would probably do something for him.'

'Do you think so?'

'I'm sure of it. We can't expect too much, of course, because Sutton's got a son of his own – '

'Oh, quite,' Mrs Reynolds said, 'though for all we see of *that* young man, he might as well not exist.'

' – but he obviously thinks a lot of Jim and I'd say he intends to do well by him.' After further thought Reynolds said: 'There's no doubt about Jim's feelings for Jane but what about Jane herself? Is she in love with him? What do you think?'

'Like you, my dear, I'm not quite sure, and I've thought it wiser not to pry. But Jane is such a sensible girl that whoever her choice may be in the end I'm quite sure it will be for the best.'

John Sutton also watched with interest the progress of Jim's courtship and, on the whole, approved of Jane.

'Prettiest thing I've seen for many a long day,' he said. 'Intelligent, too. But will she make a good wife for a working man like yourself?'

This was a difficult question for Jim to answer. Being in love with Jane he naturally assumed that she would make him a perfect wife, but he *was* only a working man and Jane was accustomed to a style of living he could not afford. Still, he had plans and certain ambitions and was by nature an optimist. He had a fair sum of money saved and he had his flock of Cotswold ewes. He earned eighteen shillings a week and there was a good, decent house which, since Oakley had gone to live in the village, was Jim's for the asking, rent free, whenever he chose to claim it. He also had his health and his strength and a good deal of drive and energy, and if Jane was willing to trust herself to him he knew he could do great things for her. But he was reluctant to talk of this to John Sutton until matters had been settled with Jane.

'I haven't actually asked her yet whether she will marry me. We've been pretty busy with haymaking, here and at Hide House, and lately I've only seen her for a short while at a time. But the work will be easing off soon and I hope I'll be able to talk to her then.'

On an evening in late July, therefore, Jim and Jane walked alone together in the hayfields at Peele where the aftermath, now that the hay had been carried, was springing up a bright soft green. Jane had been to Peele many times but never to these outlying fields and Jim pointed out the lonely barn where, thirteen years before, he had been abandoned by his uncle. Jane, who already knew the story, stood staring at the place with intensely blue eyes, her fair brows knitted in a fierce frown.

'That old place, with the fir trees behind? Weren't you frightened, being there by yourself, a little boy only ten years old, sleeping at night with the rats and the owls?'

'I hated the rats but I liked the owls. They were company in the dark. But yes, I was frightened, all the time. I was frightened of the wind in the trees, and frightened of what would become of me.'

'Your uncle was a wicked man.'

'He did me a very good turn, however, quite without intending to, for I have had a better life in Mr Sutton's care than I could ever have had otherwise.'

'I know Mr Sutton's been good to you but he says you have more than repaid him by being such a credit to him and by working so hard for him on the farm.'

They had been walking side by side, but now Jim stopped and looked at her and she met his gaze without any shyness, accepting, without embarrassment, the love he so plainly felt for her.

'Does it make any difference to you, knowing that I am a foundling?' he asked.

'Difference? What do you mean?'

'I think you must know, I'm sure you do, that I love you and want to marry you. But –'

'Oh, I see, there are *buts*!' she said, pretending to be very downcast.

'It's all a question,' he said carefully, 'of whether I am good enough for you.'

'Being a foundling?'

'Well, yes.'

'Silly,' she said, in a soft voice, and reached up to kiss him on the mouth.

His arms went round her, holding her close, and she leant against him with a little sigh, which he felt soft and warm upon his lips. It was the first time they had kissed and Jane's warm response was such that when, in a while, they drew apart, he had to take a deep breath before he was able to speak again.

'Does that mean you love me?' he asked.

'I think it must.'

'Enough to say you'll marry me?'

'Goodness! You *are* in a hurry!' she said.

'No, no, I'm not! That is – Oh, damn!' He paused a moment and began again. 'There are certain things I must tell you first. What money I earn. What my prospects are.'

'Practical things.'

'Yes, that's right.'

'You're a practical man.'

'I try to be.'

'Well, kiss me again,' Jane said, 'and then you can talk about practical things.'

As they walked together over the fields, he did his best to marshal his thoughts, and to tell her all about himself.

'I've got about twelve hundred pounds in the bank and I've got a flock of fifty sheep worth, say, another eighty pounds. I earn eighteen shillings a week – '

'Eighteen shillings! Is that all?'

'Eighteen shillings is very good. Most bailiffs get fifteen.'

'But the work you do, running the farm! You're on the go from morning to night.'

'If my wages seem little to you – and I quite see they must – I want you to know that I've got plans to rent a bit of land of my own. Nothing much to begin with, of course, but about thirty acres or so, where I can raise a few cattle and sheep and maybe fatten a pig or two.'

'Still doing your job as bailiff here? I can see you will work yourself to death if somebody doesn't stop you.'

'Oh, I can work a lot harder than that, without it killing me,' Jim said, amused. 'I'll soon show you how hard I can work, if only you will give me the chance, and one day, if all goes well, and I manage to save enough money, I shall take a really good-sized farm and set up in style as a proper farmer, independent and full-time.'

'And how long do you think that will take?'

'Ten years, perhaps. I'm not quite sure.' He turned his head to look at her. 'Do you think you could put up with being just a bailiff's wife for as long as ten years?' he asked.

'A lot depends,' Jane said gravely, 'on what a bailiff's wife has to do.'

They were now close to the old Peele farmhouse, looking down on it from above, for it lay in a slight declivity and Jim had approached it in such a way as to give Jane the best possible view. The old stonebuilt house, with its casement windows, its

61

porch overgrown with rambler roses, its walled garden and pear-hung espaliers, looked directly towards the west and now, at nine o'clock in the evening, reflected a pink sunset glow.

'That is the house,' Jim said, 'where the bailiff's wife, if she be what she ought, will spend her time looking after the bailiff.'

'Can we go inside?'

'Well, yes, we could, but I think perhaps it's wiser not. For one thing it needs a good cleaning out. For another, it's getting rather late, and if anyone saw us going in – '

'You mean my good name would be gone forever?' Jane said with a merry laugh. 'But yes, you're right, it is rather late, and it's high time I was getting home.'

Hand in hand, they walked on together, down the gently sloping fields.

'If I'm to do things properly, I ought to see your father soon and ask his permission to marry you.'

'I know what he'll say. He'll say I'm too young.'

'But at least he might let us get engaged.'

'I don't know. I'm not so sure. But I think if I spoke to him myself, I might to able to pave the way. Or I might speak to mother first . . . It's all a question of choosing the time.' Jane gave a little sigh. 'You know what parents are,' she said. 'Oh, dear! No, of course you don't, for you never had any, did you, poor boy?'

'What do you think your father will say? I'm afraid he'll think I'm not good enough for you. My prospects, such as they are – '

'Hush!' Jane said, and came to a stop, placing one finger over his lips. 'Hush! Be quiet! I've had enough!'

She leant against him, her face upturned, and he bent to kiss her on the lips. After a while she drew away.

'I really must be getting home. Will you come with me all the way? Yes, very well, but promise me this. No more talk about practical things. I'm more in the mood to be silly and gay.'

At the end of July Philip came home, lured by a letter from his father, mentioning 'interesting developments at Godsakes, concerning our friend Riddler'. And over supper that evening, with Jim also present, Sutton gave Philip the full details.

'Riddler's really done-for this time. He owes money everywhere and at least two of his creditors are threatening him with the County Court. Now, since I wrote to you, he's been served with a distraint for tithes. The collector's men were there yesterday, intending to seize Riddler's cows, – he's only got two left – but he met them at the gate with a loaded shotgun. I daresay he would have used it, too, if the men had not withdrawn. He's mad enough for anything. Anyway, that's how it is. But what is more important to us is that he's fallen behind with his mortgage dues, which should have been paid last April, and the bank has given him notice that unless the arrears are paid off by the end of next month they will be obliged to take the necessary steps. I talked to Forrester at the bank and he assured me that under no circumstances would Riddler be granted any further extension.'

'So the end is in sight, then?' Philip said.

'Yes, my boy, the end is in sight,' Sutton said, with immense satisfaction. 'It's only a matter of weeks now before Godsakes is ours at last.'

Jim, of course, already knew all this, but one detail was new to him and he strongly disapproved of it.

'Surely Forrester speaking to you like that was a breach of professional confidence?'

'He and I are old frinds,' Sutton said, 'and he knows that I have a special interest in this matter.'

'I think it was wrong, even so,' Jim said. 'I'm very glad I don't bank with him.'

Philip, lighting a cigar, was amused.

'Jim is such a moral man. At least where other people's affairs are concerned. And of course he's always been inclined to feel sorry for Morris Riddler, though I can't think why.'

'I could feel sorry for him myself if he weren't such a pig-headed fool,' Sutton said. 'But he's only hung on over there to spite me and when I think what he's done to that farm in the course of the last sixteen years – ' Sutton broke off, looking at

Jim. 'Surely you must feel pleased at the prospect of putting the place to rights? We'll be farming more than five hundred acres once we've taken Godsakes in. Surely that's something to be proud of, eh, being bailiff of such a farm?'

'For myself, yes, I can feel well pleased. I just wish that your buying Godsakes didn't involve hurting a man who has struggled so hard for so many years.'

'Well, luckily for us,' Philip said tartly, 'it isn't your business to decide.'

'Quite so,' Jim agreed, and, rising from the table, he excused himself, having work to discuss with old Abelard.

John Sutton, left alone with Philip, pushed the bottle of port towards him and watched him as he filled his glass.

'I haven't yet heard about your latest round of visits,' he said. 'Especially Langley. How is your courtship of Caroline Alton coming along?'

'It's not,' Philip said, with a certain stiffness. 'Caroline was away from home.' Then, somewhat flushed, he said: 'I'm told she is soon to become engaged to one of Colonel Conroy's sons.'

'Oh,' Sutton said, and was silent a while, watching his son with a scrutiny that was at once sympathetic and shrewd. 'Well, there are plenty of other nice girls about, and I think you may be well advised to look for one nearer home. But it seems rather as though Jim is going to pip you to the post when it comes to finding a wife.'

'Does it, though? And who's the girl?'

'Someone you haven't met,' Sutton said, 'because you've been too much away from home.'

'Imagine Jim being in love!' Philip sipped his glass of port. 'You must tell me all about it,' he said.

Out in the pasture where the flocks were grazing, Jim stood in the gathering dusk, discussing with old Abelard the next morning's work, of sorting out lambs to send to market. From across the valley came the sound of a shot and as they stood listening it was followed quite soon by another. There had been similar shots all day.

64

'That's Riddler loosing off in case the bum-bailies are lurking about,' old Abelard said grimly. 'But they will get him in the end, just as sure as eggs are eggs.'

'Yes, I'm afraid they will,' Jim said, and turned to look across the valley, imagining the feelings of the man who lived almost in a state of siege on that lonely, tumbledown farm where, in the darkness, as Jim looked, a single light came into being and burnt with a kind of stubborn defiance, faintly and dimly, in one of the windows. 'Only some kind of miracle can save Morris Riddler now, I'm afraid.'

Harvest began early in August and from then on Jim was kept fully occupied, for the acreage of corn now grown at Peele was the greatest ever, and both wheat and barley promised an exceptional yield that year. Once he went over to Hide House Farm to see the new reaping machine that Alec Reynolds had bought and while they were watching the engineer demonstrating its use in the field, Jane and her mother came out to join them and invited Jim to stay to lunch. Sadly, he was obliged to refuse, being on his way into town to draw money for the men's wages, but Jane's disappointment at his refusal sent him away almost as happy as he would have been if he could have stayed.

'Jim is a busy man, my dear,' her father said, reproving her. 'I doubt if we shall see much of him until he's finished harvesting.'

'Oh, I shan't be so very busy,' Jim said, 'that I can't walk over and see you sometimes.'

'To see us *all*?' Reynolds asked slyly. 'Or is it only one of us?'

Jim and Jane exchanged a smile.

Philip, at his father's instigation, was at this time often in Missenham, collecting information about Morris Riddler's debts, which Sutton considered might be useful to them when buying Godsakes.

One afternoon at the beginning of August, coming back from one of these errands, Philip turned off at the crossroads just outside Abbot's Lyall and rode up the lane towards Hide House Farm. It was a day of intense heat, with a hot surging wind breathing out of the east, and when he reached the River Cran he walked his mare down to the ford so that she could drink and be cool.

While he sat at ease in the saddle, looking up towards Hide House, a girl in a pale blue muslin frock, with a blue straw hat on her head, came slowly along the river bank, picking meadowsweet and wild tansy. The mare had finished drinking now but Philip, in no hurry to move, sat smiling gently to himself, watching the girl on the bank above. She had almost reached the ford when suddenly a gust of wind carried her straw hat from her head. A quick, clumsy grab; a headlong lunge; and then a small exclamation, with more than a hint of laughter in it, as the hat blew down into the river and began floating downstream.

Philip, having dismounted quickly, was just in time to reach the hat as it was floating across the ford. He fished it out and gave it a shake. The girl had now come to the top of the slip and Philip, with the hat in his hand, stood looking up at her.

'No need to ask who you are,' he said. 'I know you from my father's description.'

'Your father? Now let me see if I can guess who that is!' She studied him with her head on one side. 'No, it's no good, I just don't know. I see no likeness to anyone.'

'Then, of course, I must introduce myself.'

Leading his mare by the bridle he splashed his way across the ford and walked up to the top of the slip where the girl stood waiting for him.

'I'm Philip Sutton of Peele House Farm.' He bowed to her and proffered the hat. 'I'm afraid it's rather wet,' he said.

All through the month of August and during the first week of September, whenever Jim could spare the time from superintending the harvest at Peele, he walked over to Hide

House in the hope of seeing Jane, but each time he was disappointed. She had 'gone in to town to the dressmaker' or 'gone on a picnic with some friends to escape the heat in Lyall Woods'. Once when he called in the evening she was lying down with a sick headache, quite unable to see anyone, but when he called to enquire the next morning she had recovered sufficiently to have gone for an early morning ride by the river, 'with a party from Allern Hall'.

Jim thought it very strange that never once in all these weeks had she strolled over to see him at Peele, as she had done often enough before, but 'really her life is a whirl these days', Mrs Reynolds said to him, 'and she seems to be such a favourite, you know, with all our nice neighbours round about'.

'Yes, it would seem so,' Jim said. 'I'm glad she is better, at any rate.'

As he walked away from the house, thinking of what Mrs Reynolds had said, he became more and more aware that her manner to him had been evasive; had smacked of a certain embarrassment; had even – but maybe this was his fancy – held a hint of pity in it.

The feeling became so strong that instead of going back to Peele he went down to the river and along the bank and there, about a mile downstream, where the willows formed a shady grove, he saw Jane and Philip together, walking along, arm in arm, absorbed in each other, plainly lovers. Their horses were tethered nearby. There was no 'party from Allern Hall'; Philip and Jane were quite alone.

They did not see Jim and he stole away without showing himself. Seeing them together, so intimate, with Jane looking up into Philip's face and laughing in that particular way, although it only confirmed a fear which had been growing for days in his mind, was nevertheless a shock to him and filled him with an anger that weakened him. He felt too hurt, too vulnerable, to face them together at that moment. He needed time to be alone; to absorb the pain and to think things out.

An hour was enough. By then, instead of weakening him, his anger gave him kind a of strength. True, some faint hope lingered in his heart, causing him to ask himself whether there might, after all, be some innocent explanation of what he had seen. But he knew this hope for what it was and derided himself for his childishness. Still, he had to know for sure, and that as soon as possible. So he walked back to the narrow lane leading up to Hide House and stood in the shade of an oak tree there, waiting for Jane to return home.

When he stepped out into the lane she went rather pale and looked, just for an instant, as though she would ride right past him. But as he moved to block her way she had no choice but to stop, and when he took hold of her horse's bridle, she gave a small, nervous laugh.

'Jim! Just imagine seeing you! So early in the morning as well! I thought you were busy harvesting.'

'I've called at the house any number of times. Surely they must have told you that?'

'Oh, yes, of course they did. But I have been out a lot just lately and – '

'Jane, I must tell you,' Jim said, 'that I saw you about an hour ago with Philip Sutton at Dunton Reach.'

'Do you mean you were spying on me?'

'You can call it that if you like. But I wanted to know how I stood with you. Surely I'm entitled to that?'

Jane was suddenly close to tears, quite unable to answer him, and after a while he spoke again, quietly, in a voice well controlled. 'You said you loved me.'

'Yes. Well . . . '

'You also said you would marry me.'

'No, I didn't.' She shook her head. 'I never said any such thing.'

'But when I asked you . . . you didn't say no.'

'That's not the same as saying yes.'

'You were going to speak to your parents about it.'

'Yes. I was. But I didn't say when.'

'You mean,' he said, with some irony, 'that you may still speak to them even now?'

'No. Not now.'

'Why not?' he asked.

'You know why not.'

68

'Yes, I know. Because something better has come along.'

'I suppose it's only natural that you should feel like this about it – '

'I certainly can't imagine anyone feeling any differently.'

'Jim, I'm sorry. Truly I am. I didn't mean to hurt you like this.'

'Are you going to marry him?'

'Yes.'

'In that case there's nothing more to be said – except for one or two things I shall have to say to Philip himself.'

'What things?' Jane asked.

But Jim was already walking away, impatient now to get back to Peele.

Philip stood in the stable doorway, talking to Charlie Clements who was inside, grooming the mare. He turned as Jim came into the yard and sauntered towards him, tapping his boot with his riding-crop.

'My father is out looking for you. Nobody seemed to know where you were.'

'I've just come from seeing Jane.'

'Ah,' Philip said, and his gaze sharpened, becoming wary, inquisitive, amused, and full of bright expectancy. 'Jane. Yes. Exactly so.'

'She tells me she's going to marry you.'

'Then, of course, it must be true.'

'You haven't wasted much time,' Jim said. 'You've only been home a month or so.'

'Five weeks and three days, to be precise.'

'And never once in that time have you even mentioned meeting her.'

'There was a good reason for that.'

'I can well believe it,' Jim said.

'I was trying to spare your feelings, you see, because, right from the very start, I loved the girl and she loved me.'

'Loving people,' Jim said, 'is something she seems to find easy to do.'

'That is not a very gentlemanly remark.'

'I'm not feeling gentlemanly.'

'No, I can see you're not.'

'But then, I am not a gentleman, nor have I ever laid claim to be.'

'No?' Philip said, with a lift of his brows. 'And yet you expected to marry Jane, a girl of good family connections, not to mention superior breeding.' He spread his hands in disbelief. 'You, a farm bailiff,' he continued, 'earning eighteen shillings a week, hoping to lure the poor girl into marriage with your few paltry hundreds in the bank and your talk of renting a little farm –'

Philip, though watching so warily, was nevertheless taken by surprise when Jim suddenly lashed out and caught him a stinging, back-handed blow on the mouth. Until this moment Jim's feelings had been kept under control but now, as he learnt that his cherished ambitions had been discussed between Philip and Jane, and made the subject of ridicule between them, he allowed his anger a free rein and when Philip, with a muttered exclamation, cut at him with his riding-crop, Jim struck out straight and hard with his fist and sent Philip sprawling on his back on the cobbles.

Behind him, in the stable doorway, Charlie Clements now appeared, but before he could intervene John Sutton walked into the yard.

'What the devil's going on?'

Philip got slowly to his feet.

'Jim,' he said, nursing his jaw, 'has just found out that I am going to marry Jane Reynolds.'

'You are going to do what?'

'And, as you see, he's not taking it well. He's no kind of sportsman, I'm afraid. That's one thing we've never drummed into him.'

'All right, Clements, get on with your work! There's no need to stand gaping there!' Sutton, very red in the face, waited until Clements had gone before turning back to Philip. 'When did all this happen with Jane? It's all very sudden, isn't it? You've only been home a few weeks.'

'So everyone keeps telling me. But a few weeks is all it took.' Philip stood brushing the dust from his clothes. 'You have said often enough that it was time I married and settled down and that is what I'm planning to do. It just happens that the girl in question is one Jim thought he had a lien on and now that he finds himself mistaken – '

'Well, it can't be settled by fighting like a couple of stable-boys.' Sutton glanced questioningly at Jim. 'If the girl has made her choice – '

'Oh, yes, she's made her choice,' Jim said, with great bitterness, 'but you mustn't be surprised if I'm not very ready in offering my felicitations.'

'I'm not pretending to be surprised. I'd feel exactly the same as you do. But this is no place to discuss the matter. We'd all be better indoors.'

'I'm not in a mood for discussion,' Jim said. 'I think I'd be better left alone. Anyway, there's work to be done, and I had better get on with it, doing my duty as your bailiff, earning my eighteen shillings a week!'

He strode away, out of the yard, and Sutton turned again to his son. 'Come indoors,' he said tersely. 'I've got a few things to say to you.'

At about half-past ten that morning, at work in the rickyard, Jim received word that he was wanted up at the house. He went somewhat reluctantly and found Sutton alone in his study.

'This is a bad business, Jim, and I am more sorry than I can say. I've had it out with Philip and I've told him what I think of him. But it seems he's perfectly serious about wanting to marry Jane and there's no changing his mind about it.'

'How could that possibly help anything? You surely don't think I would want her now, when she's made it plain that she doesn't want me?'

'No. Of course not. I didn't mean that.'

Sutton, sitting behind his desk, motioned Jim into a chair, but Jim, refusing, continued to stand, his fists buried deep in his jacket pockets.

'Philip tells me,' Sutton said, 'that they intend to marry quite soon.'

Jim said nothing, but stood like a stone.

'In fact they talk of an autumn wedding. Early October, perhaps, he says. It all seems very quick to me, but there it is. You will have to consider what to do.'

'Do?' Jim queried. 'Why, what would I do?'

'Well, you can't very well stay here after this, and surely you wouldn't want to? With Philip and Jane living here and such bad blood between you and him . . . it's out of the question, you must surely see that?'

'You mean I would have to move out of the house? Yes, of course, I do see that.'

'Not just out of the house, but away from Peele altogether. Somewhere new. Fresh woods, as they say. I'm sorry about it. Angry, too. You're a good lad and I'm fond of you and your work here as bailiff these past three years – '

'Am I to be turned off, then?' Jim said.

'That's not the way I would put it, myself, but you must certainly leave Peele, and the sooner it can be arranged, the better it will be for everyone. I've given it a good deal of thought and the ideal solution, it seems to me, is for you to go out to Canada and join my cousin Tom on his farm. He badly needs young men like you and if I write to him straight away – '

'Canada!' Jim said hollowly, and, with a wry twist of his mouth, he asked, 'Is that quite far enough away, do you think?'

'It will mean a new life for you, my boy. A whole new adventure. A challenge, that's what! Tom farms five thousand acres out there in Ontario. Five thousand acres, just think of that! Miles and miles of nothing but corn! It will be a splendid chance for you to make a new start and I'm sure you will agree with me that it will be better for everyone if you were gone clean away before Philip's wedding to Jane takes place. In fact, as soon as it can be fixed. It'll spare your own feelings and theirs.'

'Whatever I do,' Jim said, 'it will not be to spare Philip's feelings.'

'I understand how you feel but – he is my son, remember.'

72

'And I am nobody's son. I've got no family of my own. No money to speak of. No land, no home. Nothing to offer but what I am.'

'And a very good bargain, too,' Sutton said, 'for the right girl in the right place.'

Jim's face remained clenched, his eyes a cold, glittering blue, and Sutton, looking up at him, gave a small, sympathetic sigh. But he was anxious to have Jim's answer; anxious to get his plan under way; and he spoke now with a touch of impatience.

'Well? What do you say to my idea? Canada is a wonderful place, you know, and it's crying out for young chaps like you. You'll make good there in no time at all. So what do you say? Shall I write to Tom?'

Jim suddenly turned to the door.

'I'll think about it and let you know.'

Chapter Six

Once again Jim needed to think and this time, driven by some primitive instinct, he climbed the slopes of Luton Camp; first the gently sweeping slopes, divided roughly into fields; then the higher, steeper slopes, where the turf was worn away in places, revealing the pale stone beneath, which crumbled under his feet as he climbed.

When he got to the top of the hill he sat on a low grassy mound, underneath a hawthorn tree, and looked down on the valley below. He could see almost everything from this height and everything he saw was dear to him, so that the thought of leaving it caused an angry ache in his heart. In the confusion of his mind it was impossible for him to tell which caused him the most pain: his banishment or the reason behind it; because both these things were so twisted together that contemplation of the one only magnified the hurt of the other.

His sense of betrayal filled him completely, for fate had struck him a two-fold blow and the knowledge that he had no rights in the matter only increased his bitterness. Of course, John Sutton was right: he would certainly not want to stay at Peele; but his lack of choice made him squirm all the same, inducing a fierce rebelliousness in him, and it was this aspect of things – the fact that the whole of his future life was being thus decided out of hand – that made him reject Sutton's plan for sending him to Ontario.

This rejection cleared his mind. The feeling that he was a helpless pawn in a game being played by other men was thus removed at a single stroke leaving room for his rebellion to grow. He saw that although his plans had been spoilt, his life was nevertheless his own to direct and govern as he chose. And as he sat looking down on the valley, comparing the rich, productive lands of Peele, so neat and well cared for, just below, with the rough, neglected, tumbledown sprawl of Godsakes over on the other side, he saw that he could use his life in a way that would not only further his own ambitions but defeat the Suttons in one of theirs.

The idea came to him not in a flash but quietly, almost cunningly, as though it had lain in his mind for some time, developing there, secretly, until it had grown to be part of himself and only awaited recognition. For it came to him whole, this idea of his, and brought with it such a sense of purpose that his pain and anger were transmuted at once into strength and energy. The destructive force in him, that wanted to smash and annihilate, was replaced by a creative force that wanted to mend, restore, rebuild. And as he examined this idea, with all its many implications, he was filled with a subtle kind of excitement. Something immense was growing in him and he made it welcome, allowing it to take possession of his heart and his mind.

He had lost something of himself that day, on learning that Jane was playing him false in a way that took no account of his feelings for her, or of his pride. But now he had found another self, harder, tougher than the first, and he felt the stirrings of a fierce impatience, wanting to put this new self to the test and show the world what it could do.

Impatience brought him to his feet and he set off quickly down the hill, slithering over the loose, broken stones and sending them rattling down the slope until, reaching the regular path, he forced himself to a steadier pace. His plan as yet needed much careful thought and there were details to be worked out before he reached Godsakes Farm.

Morris Riddler had been served with an official County Court notice, three days before, informing him that an Order of Possession had been granted against the property known as Godsakes Farm in favour of Messrs Martin and Moore, bankers, of Missenham, in the county of Gloucester, and that the said property would, in default of payment of certain debts and dues, set out in detail below, be put up for sale by Public Auction on Monday 27 September 1858.

On being served the notice, he had first read it, then torn it up, telling the officer who had delivered it that 'anyone who comes here trying to put my farm up for sale will get a skitter of shot in his backside.' There was little or no work to do on the farm at this time because the only remaining stock consisted of two cows, one of them dry, and some two or three dozen hens. The labourers, Lovell and Smith, had been laid off all through the summer, though they still occupied their cottages, and Riddler's whole day was now spent patrolling the farm, on the alert for marauders.

He had seen Jim coming from a long way off and was at the gate, waiting for him, shotgun nestling in the crook of his arm, suspicion written across his face.

'What do you want?' he asked with a growl.

'I've got a proposition to put to you.'

'If the Suttons sent you, you can go to hell.'

'This is nothing to do with the Suttons. This is business of my own. They don't know I've come.'

'Since when have you had business that wasn't connected with the Suttons?'

'Since today,' Jim replied.

Riddler cocked an eyebrow at him, giving him a long, hard look.

'Something wrong between you and them?'

'Yes.'

'Maybe I can guess what it is. I hear the gossip, you know, now and then. And rumour reached me recently that you and Philip Sutton were both after the same girl.'

'In that case you knew before I did myself.'

'Well, since you've fallen out with the Suttons and haven't come on their behalf, I don't mind hearing what you have to say.' Riddler opened the ramshackle gate. 'You'd better come into the house,' he said.

The farmhouse kitchen was very bare. A table, three chairs, and a Welsh dresser were the only furniture in the room, and these were shabby to a degree. But Jim was not surprised at this for it was common knowledge in the district that every saleable thing at Godsakes had been sold to pay Riddler's debts.

Kirren, who was cleaning the stone-flagged floor with a broom dipped into a bucket of water, stopped and looked up in surprise at seeing Riddler enter with Jim. She leant on her broom, frowning at him, and, sharing her father's first suspicions, only barely answered his nod. Riddler stood his gun in a corner, clumped over the wet flags, and sat down in a chair at the table, motioning Jim to do the same.

'You know my daughter, Kirren?' he said, and, over his shoulder, to Kirren herself: 'This is Jim Lundy from Peele.'

'I know perfectly well who it is.'

'You needn't take that tone with him. He hasn't come to turn us out. Or so he assures me, anyway.' Riddler, sitting sideways in his chair, one arm resting on the table, looked at Jim sitting opposite. 'A proposition, I think you said?'

'Yes, that's right.'

'Well, fire away.'

'I'll make no bones about it,' Jim said. 'You're done-for here. We both know that. And it's only a matter of two or three weeks before the farm is sold over your head. Your loan at the bank still stands at a little over six hundred pounds – you can guess how I come by that information – but it is your payments on the loan, and a few other debts elsewhere, that are your most pressing problem, and if you could only settle them you would be in the clear again.'

'Two hundred pounds! That's all I need! And because I can't find it they'll sell me up!' Riddler exclaimed bitterly. But he was narrowly watching Jim and in his small, screwed-up eyes there was already a gleam of hope. 'But maybe you've come along with some miraculous solution such as I've been praying for?'

'I've come to offer to pay your debts.'

'Have you, by God?' Riddler breathed, and turned his head to glance at Kirren, who, still holding her broom, was standing in silence nearby. 'And in return – what do you want?'

77

'A share in the farm.'

'What sort of a share?'

'A partnership. Half and half.'

'Just for paying off my debts?'

'No, there's more to it than that,' Jim said. 'I've got twelve hundred pounds in the bank, my savings over thirteen years. I've also got my flock, as you know, worth perhaps eighty pounds. I propose using my money to pay off your debts and re-stock the farm, keeping a certain amount back to cover all the running expenses, such as the men's wages and so on. We then work together to build it up, and in return, when that is achieved, a half share of the farm will be mine, plus a half share of the profits, of course.'

Jim, sitting upright in his chair, turned and half looked at Riddler's daughter, not to win any comment from her but because he was irritated by the way she stood just out of sight behind him. He then turned to face Riddler again.

'That's my proposition,' he said. 'Details would have to be worked out, of course, and some kind of legal agreement drawn up. But, in a nutshell, that's about it.'

'You don't expect much, do you, by God, in exchange for your twelve hundred pounds? Have you any idea, I wonder, how much it cost me to buy this place?'

'Yes, it cost you three thousand pounds, plus the interest on your loan. But you wouldn't get half that sum for it now, being so run-down as it is, and if my twelve hundred pounds is enough to put you into production again, it's surely worth more to you than just its value, counted as coin? Anyway, I propose earning the rest of my share by working and putting the farm to rights, and as that will take a good many years –'

'All right, all right, you've made your point! But I don't much fancy sharing a farm that I've had to myself for thirty-six years.'

'In that case you'll lose it altogether,' Jim said. 'You can't fight the law for ever, even with a shotgun, and when the sale takes place, the farm will go to the highest bidder. And that, as you know, will be John Sutton.'

'Yes, you've got me there, haven't you? Because you know

damned well I'd do just about anything rather than see him get my farm. But go on with your proposition. There's one or two things to account for yet. What happens, for instance, when I die? My share of the farm will be Kirren's then. Do you propose being partners with *her?*'

'By that time, all being well, the farm will be on its feet again and I shall be able to buy her out.'

There was a silence in the room; a silence that lasted a long time; and throughout it Riddler's keen, bright gaze remained fixed on Jim's face. At last, however, he stirred in his chair, twisting round to look at Kirren.

'What do *you* think about it?' he asked.

Kirren shrugged. 'It seems a good enough plan,' she said, 'up to the point where I get turned out.'

'*Bought* out, not turned out,' Jim said.

'It means the same thing, doesn't it? I still lose my home.'

Her words surprised him. Gave him pause. Until today, he had never met the girl face to face. He had only seen her in the distance, at haymaking time in the meadows, perhaps, or trudging along the road in to town, taking her produce to the market. But he knew what her life had been like on this farm and he had assumed that she would welcome a plan that offered some chance of escape.

'Does the place mean so much to you, then?'

'I'm not sure what it means to me. I've never thought about it till now. But this is the only home I've ever known and God knows I've worked hard enough for it, helping my father keep hold of it.'

'You'll be repaid for that work in the end because when I buy your share of the farm you'll be able to rent a cottage somewhere and probably have enough money to make you independent for life.'

'On the other hand,' she said, 'if everything goes as well as you think, and the farm begins making money again, I could in the end buy you out instead.'

'Oh, no, I wouldn't want that!' Jim said, emphatically. 'I would want the farm for myself.'

Riddler, having listened intently to this exchange, now

79

spoke again. 'Why should you want the farm so much? To spite John Sutton and his son? To show that girl at Hide House what a prize she's lost in jilting you?'

'I don't think my reasons matter,' Jim said, 'but certainly I would want the farm.'

'Seems we all want it,' Riddler said. 'We are united in that at least. But there is one problem in your plan. Supposing I was to drop dead before the farm was paying its way? You wouldn't be able to buy Kirren's share then. You'd both have to stick it out here together and that wouldn't do at all. It wouldn't be decent. Folk would talk.'

Jim became silent. He was badly put out. It seemed to him unbelievable that such a foolish, irrelevant problem should threaten the working-out of his plan. But before he could frame any kind of answer, Morris Riddler was speaking again.

'Your plan is fine as far as it goes but you haven't thought it through to the end. I reckon the best way of making it work is for you and Kirren to get married. That way you get hold of the farm without having to turn her out and it does away with any need for complicated legal arrangements. The lawyers have had enough money out of me in the past. I'm damned if I'll let them have any more.'

Jim and Kirren both stared at him.

'You're surely not serious?' Jim said.

'Oh, yes, I am.'

'Then I'm afraid you must think again, because marriage is quite out of the question. It doesn't come into my plans at all.'

'Nor mine,' Kirren said. 'I thought I'd made that plain enough.'

'You be quiet,' Riddler said, 'and listen to what I have to say.'

'I don't care what you've got to say! I've heard it often enough before. I am *not* going to marry anyone – neither this man here nor any other – just to please you and keep the farm.'

'Please me be damned!' Riddler said. 'It's *you* I'm thinking of, not myself.'

'I can't think why,' Kirren said. 'You never have done in the past.'

'I'm talking about the future now – when I'm dead and in my grave and you're left with no one to take care of you.'

'I can take care of myself.'

'I doubt if you'll get another chance of a husband falling into your lap –'

'How many times do I have to tell you that a husband is the last thing I want?' Kirren, with angry impatience, dipped her broom into the bucket and began brushing the flagstones again, sweeping the water towards the door. 'To saddle myself with the kind of life my mother endured with you all those years? Oh dear me no! I'd sooner be dead!'

The violence of Kirren's outburst had a strange effect on Jim. It gave him a stab of perverse pleasure, enhancing, in a peculiar way, his own dark disillusionment. And, looking at her more closely now, he saw her as though for the first time. Riddler, catching this look of his, shrewdly waited a while in silence, guessing the nature of the young man's thoughts. Then, judging his moment, he said:

'Well, I don't know, I'm sure! But seeing you're both so set against marriage it seems to me you're ideally suited. Made for each other! The perfect match! So why not look on it as a business arrangement, purely for the sake of the farm, without any strings on either side? You say you would want the whole farm for yourself but if you bought Kirren out you'd only have to get someone else to cook and clean and keep house for you. Now you may not think it to look at her but Kirren is a very good housekeeper and you couldn't do better than keep her on.'

'High praise indeed!' Kirren said, speaking as though to the broom in her hands.

'And one thing about a wife is, you don't have to pay her a wage,' Riddler said.

'Ah,' Kirren said, with a little nod, 'and there we come to the heart of it!'

But she had stopped sweeping again and was now looking directly at Jim. Their eyes met in a straight, steady stare; with a curious kind of hostile reserve; but this hostility, in a strange way, somehow formed a bond between them, perhaps because its cause lay, not in their two separate selves, but in the person of Morris Riddler. They had known each other by sight for years but they met today for the first time. They were strangers, the pair of them, and while they frankly appraised each other, both understood perfectly that strangers was how they wished to remain.

Quietly, cautiously, Jim spoke to her.

'Purely as a business arrangement, exactly as your father suggests, would you be willing to consider it?'

'I don't know,' Kirren said. 'Would you?'

'A formality only? Just a marriage in name? It does seem to make some sense, I think, and there's no doubt it would simplify matters when it comes to joint ownership of the farm.'

'Oh, it would simplify matters most beautifully,' Kirren said in a dry tone, 'for a wife has almost no rights whatever in matters concerning property.'

'Yes, well, I suppose that's true. But a wife does have rights of a kind, after all. For one thing she is entitled to expect that her husband will always do well by her. And that, even in a marriage of convenience, is a duty I would most certainly fulfil.'

'No strings attached, as my father suggests?'

'None whatever,' Jim said. 'I would make no demands on you as a husband. In fact, where our personal lives are concerned, we should be scarcely more to each other than we are now.'

Kirren, it seemed, still had her doubts.

'How do I know I can trust you?'

'You don't,' he said bluntly, meeting her gaze. 'But it is scarcely the kind of matter on which I can swear an affidavit, is it?'

Riddler, watching Kirren's face, gave a cynical laugh.

'You can always lock your door, girl. That's simple enough, surely?' he said. 'And if Jim is worried on the same score, he can lock his!'

'Your daughter needs time to think,' Jim said, 'and so, for that matter, do I.'

'All right,' Riddler said. 'But that's my condition – no marriage, no deal.'

'You are hardly in a position to make conditions.'

'No, maybe not,' Riddler said. 'But I'm making this one all the same. And if you want this farm as badly as I think you do, then *you're* in no position to turn it down. Now come with me and I'll show you round. You'll see what you will be taking on and Kirren will have time to think.'

It was seven years since Jim had set foot on Godsakes land and in those seven years its ruination had been complete. In every field it was the same: a wilderness of rank grass and weeds, with clumps of thorn and briar here and there, and hedges so badly neglected that the timber in them stood twenty feet high and brambles spread out over the headlands forming thickets twenty feet wide. No land had been ploughed in recent years and Riddler's ploughs, together with other implements, lay under a heap of junk in a corner of the crumbling barn. All the farm buildings were in disrepair and, like the land itself, were infested with every kind of vermin. The pig-pens and sties were choke-full with nettles and more than half the hen-coops were fit for nothing but firewood.

'A sight for sore eyes, eh?' Riddler said. 'And all Sutton's fault, every bit of it. This was a good farm once but when I was given the chance to buy and Sutton ran up the price like that . . . But there, you know the tale well enough, so there's no point in dragging it out again. But I can never forgive him for that and never will so long as I live, because that big loan has dragged me down. It's like as if I were stuck in the mire – the more I struggled, the deeper I sank. Now if only my son Eddy had lived . . . But it's no good thinking of things like that and maybe I'll get a son-in-law instead. Not quite the same as a son of my own, but a whole heap better than nothing at all.'

The two men came to a halt. Their tour had brought them back to the yard and they leant together over the gate, watching the few scrawny hens pecking about in the dust.

'Well, now you've seen all there is to see, what do you think?' Riddler said. 'Think you can make a go of it? Pull it together, like you said? There's still the damned mortgage, remember – six hundred pounds to be paid off yet, plus the interest at four per cent. D'you think, with that millstone round your neck, you can pull the farm back on its feet and get it to pay its way again?'

'Yes, if you let me have a free hand, to run things my way, as I think best.'

'Oh, so you're to have all the say, are you, and I'm to stand by, clapping my hands?'

'We should discuss things together, of course, as any business partners would.'

'Discusss things between us,' Riddler said, 'and then do exactly what you decide.'

'You've made the decisions up to now and as a result the farm has failed.'

'It's not my fault the farm has failed! I've had the devil's own bad luck these past sixteen years and damn well you know it too –'

'Yes, I know it well enough, but as it will be my money we shall be using to start the farm working again –'

'All right, all right, don't rub it in!' Riddler said with an angry scowl. 'Who pays the piper calls the tune. There's no arguing against that. And if you think you can pull it off . . . '

'Don't you believe me?'

'Yes, I do. I've got to believe it, there's no other hope. I know you can work – I've seen it myself. And you've got your head screwed on pretty well – you wouldn't be Sutton's bailiff else. If anyone can pull the place together, I reckon it's you. You'll get your free hand, right enough, and if it means keeping Sutton out . . . Well, I don't need to tell you, but I'd give a great deal to make sure of that.' He turned his head to look at Jim and after a little while he said: 'It seems as though, from the way you're talking, you've made up your mind to accept my condition.'

'Yes, I accept it,' Jim said.

'So,' Riddler said, quietly, and the word came out in a little hiss. 'It all depends on Kirren, then. Let's go and see what she says.'

Kirren was standing in the back porchway. She seemed to be looking out for them.

'Well, miss? Have you made up your mind?'

'Yes,' Kirren said. She looked at Jim. 'If he agrees to it, so do I.'

'Of course he damn well agrees to it! Can't you see by the look on his face? There aren't any flies on this young chap. He sees the good sense of my idea and I'm glad to find, now you're put to it, that you've got the nous to see it, too.'

Riddler was now cock-a-hoop. He could scarcely contain himself. Boisterously, he turned to Jim and clapped one heavy hand on his back, at the same time taking Kirren's arm and giving it a long, hard squeeze.

'Come indoors, the pair of you! We've still got a few things to sort out yet. And if there's anything left in the bottle we'll drink damnation to the Suttons!'

Just after two o'clock Jim returned to Peele House, quietly mounted the stairs to his room, and put his clothes and other belongings into an old canvas satchel. With this slung on his shoulder he went downstairs and was crossing the hall to Sutton's study when Mrs Abelard came out of the dining-room. Her face clouded at sight of him, especially when she noted the satchel, and, taking his arm, she led him aside, speaking to him in an undertone.

'There's been an upset, hasn't there, about your young lady at Hide House Farm?'

'Yes, Abby. It's all gone wrong. She doesn't want me after all.' Jim had thought himself strong and hard but under the old woman's scrutiny he felt himself a boy again and there was a tremor in his voice as he said: 'She's going to marry Philip instead.'

'Mr Philip has stolen her from you. That's how it is, you mark my words. He was always that way inclined, even when you were boys together. But a girl who changes her mind as easy as that isn't worth bothering about and I'd say she's a lot better matched to Mr Philip than she would be to you.'

Jim said nothing and the old housekeeper, seeing his face, clicked her tongue, much vexed with herself.

'Tchah! What a thing for me to say! As though that was any comfort to you!' Once again she took hold of his arm, distressed for him, at a loss for words. 'And are you leaving us, then, for good?'

'Yes, I'm not wanted here any more. Nor, come to that, do I want to stay. But I shan't be going far, Abby. Just across the valley, that's all.'

'Across the valley?' Abby gaped. 'Whatever do you mean by that, Mr Jim?'

Jim's explanation was cut short because, quietly though he and Abby had talked, John Sutton had heard them and now, opening his study door, he looked out into the hall. Discreetly, the old woman withdrew, vanishing into her kitchen, and Jim turned towards Sutton, who came across the hall to him.

'What's this?' he asked with a frown, touching the satchel on Jim's back.

'I thought, since you wanted me to leave, I might as well go straight away. The sooner the better, I think you said, and I am rather inclined to agree. But I'm not going to Ontario. I'm going to Godsakes instead.'

'Godsakes?' Sutton said blankly, and then, with quick-growing suspicion, 'What the devil do you mean?'

'I'm going to pay Riddler's debts. We shall be partners, he and I, and we'll work together to pull up the farm. I've just been over there, bargaining with him, and now I'm going back – for good.'

'My God! You would do that to me?' Sutton was crimson in the face. 'You know I've always wanted that farm! You know I've waited sixteen years!'

'Yes, I know it very well, just as Philip knew I wanted Jane.'

'All this fuss over a girl! A pretty face! A pair of blue eyes! Dammit, Jim, just look at yourself! You're a young man of twenty-four and you've got enough about you, in the way of looks and ability, to take your pick from a dozen girls. In a few months from now you'll have got over this business with Jane and you'll have no trouble, believe me, when it comes to finding another wife.'

86

'I've already found one,' Jim said. 'I'm going to marry Kirren Riddler.'

'Riddler's daughter?'

'Yes, that's right.'

'But you don't even know the wretched girl!'

'It would seem I didn't know Jane, either, for all I understood of her.'

'My God!' Sutton exclaimed. 'Do you mean you are marrying her just to get hold of Godsakes Farm? A marriage like that won't bring you much joy!'

'No, well, you may be right. But we'll see how much joy Philip's marriage brings him.'

'I never thought to see the day when you would do a thing like this to me.'

'The day,' Jim said, with irony, 'has brought surprises for both of us.'

'After all I've done for you, giving you a home all these years! Bringing you up and caring for you, almost as though you were my son!'

'You've always been very good to me and I thank you for it,' Jim said. 'But now, although I've done nothing wrong, you would like to be rid of me. You would send me away to Canada, a place where I have no wish to be, and no doubt, if you had the power, you would rub me clean off the face of the earth. Well, I am not to be got rid of so easily, simply because, through no fault of my own, I have become an embarrassment to you. Common nobody I may be but I still have the right to run my own life and that is what I intend to do.'

Following these words Jim became silent, looking straight into Sutton's eyes and seeing there a burning reflection of his own anger and bitterness. Then, with some awkwardness, he said: 'I'm sorry it's ending like this. You've been a good friend to me until now. But after what's happened today, well, I can never feel quite the same way again and I know that my going to Godsakes will put paid to our friendship once and for all.'

'You are going, though, in spite of that?'

'Yes.'

'I suppose it's your idea of revenge.'

'Whatever it is,' Jim said, 'Philip is the one who's to blame for it.'

A few minutes later, with his long shepherding stick in his hand and his dog, Jess, close at his heels, he was crossing the stable yard, on his way to the gate leading into the pastures. He had his hand on the sneck of the gate when Sutton came out of the house and stood in the open doorway.

'Where do you think you're going?'

'I'm going up to fetch my flock and say goodbye to old Abelard.'

Jim passed through the gate and set off up the fields and Sutton, still red in the face, stood staring grimly after him.

Philip, who had been at Hide House lunching with Jane and her parents, returned to Peele in time to see Jim driving his flock over one of the little bridges spanning the brook in the valley bottom. Finding his father in the front drive, where a good view could be had of the valley, he asked what was going on and in a few pithy sentences Sutton explained.

'Paying Riddler's debts?' Philip repeated. 'To stop us getting Godsakes Farm?'

'He not only stops us getting it, but he gets it himself, damn his eyes, for he's marrying Riddler's daughter, he says.'

'Marrying – ? Is this a joke?'

'No, it is not!' Sutton snapped. 'He's in deadly earnest, I promise you.'

'But,' Philip said, floundering, 'he can't possibly make it pay. He hasn't got the capital. Oh, I know he's got some money saved, but not a fraction of what he will need to put that farm in order again – '

'Maybe not. But what he's got is quite enough to keep the place from being sold for another sixteen years or so and by that time I may well be dead. As for not making a go of it, I wouldn't even be too sure of that, because Jim is a very determined young man. Clever, too. He uses his head.'

'It would take him half his life – '

'So what if it does? What's that to him? He is only twenty-

88

four. What better thing could he do with his life than spend it in reclaiming that land?'

'You think it's a possibility, then, that he will make a success of it?' Philip's face was now thunderous. 'And yet you stand here quietly, letting him take those sheep off the farm!'

'The sheep are his. He bought them himself.'

'With money you gave him, don't forget.'

'What's given is given,' Sutton said. 'It can't be taken back.'

'I'm not so sure about that. I think we should see old Kelloway. Those sheep were raised on our land and I'm sure if we took it to law – '

'Oh, be quiet, you stupid fool! Even if we did have a claim on those sheep, how would the story sound, do you think, once it got round the neighbourhood? What sort of name should we have after that? What would people think of us?'

'Good God, it's monstrous!' Philip exclaimed. 'To think of his sneaking off like that and doing a deal with the likes of Riddler just to vent his spite on us! After what we've done for him over the past fourteen years – '

' "We"?' Sutton said, in a scathing tone. 'And what have *you* ever done for him, apart from taking his girl away from him?' Then, with a quick gesture, he said, 'Oh, never mind! Let it pass, let it pass! For heaven's sake, don't let us two quarrel as well, otherwise where shall we be? But it is a pity all the same that out of all the girls in the district you had to fix your fancy on Jane. It's lost us Godsakes, there's no doubt of that.' Sutton turned to go into the house, but paused just long enough to lay a hand on Philip's shoulder and to say, with a touch of dryness: 'Let's hope she turns out to be worth it, eh?'

Down in the bottom of the valley Jim's sheep had now crossed the meadows and he was letting them through a gate that led into Godsakes land. From the top of the main farm track Riddler and Kirren stood watching as the neatly bunched flock of fifty ewes came slowly up the sloping fields with the young man and the dog behind.

The sight of these golden-fleeced sheep affected Morris Riddler deeply, for no such first-class stock as this had been seen at Godsakes for many years, and the surge of emotion was so strong in him that when he suddenly turned to Kirren his queer, crooked, shapeless face was lit with a kind of holy joy and, at the same time, wet with tears.

'Look at them, Kirrie! Just look at them! Did you ever see anything so beautiful in all your born days? Why, that old saying, the Golden Hoof, was never truer than it is for us here today, because that little flock of Cotswold Lions means that this farm is in business again!'

Even Kirren herself was affected and although her glance was sardonic, as always, there was nevertheless a smile on her lips and a gleam of living hope in her eyes. For once she and her father were in accord, sharing the same feelings and thoughts, and he, aware of this sympathy between them, suddenly clasped her in his arms, pressing her head against his chest and giving a little sobbing laugh. Just as suddenly he released her and, with his clumsy, lumbering gait, set off down the track to meet Jim.

Usually dinner at Godsakes was eaten at noon but because of events that day it was almost four o'clock when three people instead of two sat down to eat their first meal together.

'You won't find us delicate here,' Riddler said. 'Plain boiled bacon and cabbage and taters, that's what we live on, Kirren and me. You will find it a bit of a change after the way you've lived at Peele.'

'Plain food is good enough for me,' Jim said.

But the boiled bacon was terrible stuff. The smell of it as he sat down to eat told him what to expect and although he tried to harden himself, at the first mouthful of tainted meat, with its thick coating of rancid fat, his gorge rose in such a way that it required an effort of will to chew the mouthful and swallow it. Taking a generous helping of salt before attacking the meat again, he saw that Kirren was watching him.

'You don't have to eat it,' she said. 'It can go back in the pot.'

'If you can eat it, so can I.'

'We're used to it. You're not.'

Riddler ate stolidly, leaning low over his plate, watching Jim with open amusement.

'You may as well get used to it. There's a tidy bit of it left yet.' He pointed up at the rack in the rafters, on which were laid the whole of one flitch and the half of another, each tightly covered in muslin, each with its dark cluster of flies. 'That old pig was the last we raised. I'll tell you how he came to die.'

The story of how the pig had died did not make it any easier for Jim to finish eating his meal and when at last he laid down his knife and fork it was with a sense of relief that did not go unnoticed by Riddler.

'Think you'll live after that?' he asked. 'Think you'll survive it, do you, eh?'

Jim rose and pushed in his chair.

'I'm going for another walk round the farm.'

'Hang on a minute. I'll come with you.'

'Thanks, but I'd sooner be alone. I've got some thinking to do.'

Looking around the farm again, noting things that had to be done, he could scarcely wait for the morning, so impatient was he to begin. But his first task in the morning would be to go in to town with Riddler and arrange for the payment of his debts, beginning with the mortgage dues, and as it would be market day his second most important task would be to buy new stock for the farm.

But all the time, as he laid his plans, other thoughts were troubling him, and the source of these was the girl, Kirren. He was fretted by feelings of guilt, asking himself what he was doing marrying a girl he cared nothing for; a girl who was so much a stranger to him that until today they had never even spoken together.

For himself he had no regrets; only a bitter satisfaction at taking such a cold-blooded step, as though he would demonstrate to himself and the world that *that* was all marriage meant to him now. One wife would do as well as another. What did it matter who she was? He would never now want to marry for love. He would not succumb to *that* weakness again. And although Kirren was a stranger to him, at least he knew where he was with her, for there could be no betrayal where there had been no promise of love.

But Kirren herself – what of her? Was he not doing wrong, taking advantage of her poverty? Hadn't he, at her father's instigation, pushed her into this doubtful transaction merely to further his own ends, without proper consideration for her feelings, as a girl, as a woman? These questions gnawed at his mind and when he returned to the house and found Kirren alone in the kitchen he broached the subject immediately.

She heard him out in silence, looking at him searchingly, her eyes very dark under frowning brows, and when he had finished she asked bluntly:

'Are you having second thoughts?'

'For myself – no. For you – yes, perhaps. I feel I haven't considered you enough. I've been thinking too much about myself. I feel you've been thrust into this thing without having enough time to think.'

'I'm not a fool. I know what I'm doing. You said you didn't want a proper marriage and I said I felt the same, so as long as we both mean what we say – '

'Don't you want children?'

'No. I do not.'

'Most women do.'

'How do you know?'

'Well,' he said, uncertainly, 'it's an understood thing, I would have thought.'

'When women marry, they generally have children whether they like it or not. They're given no choice in the matter. They just have to make the best of it. But I don't intend that to happen to me because I wouldn't want to bring a child into the world. Another life, another soul . . . And to be responsible for raising it . . . That thought is frightening to me.'

'Frightening?' Jim asked. 'But surely if a man and a woman love one another – '

'Yes? What?'

'Nothing,' he said, with a shake of his head. The subject was painful to him; he had stumbled thus far unwittingly. 'Nothing. Never mind.'

'I've heard my father say that he loved my mother, but he had a queer way of showing it, driving her into the grave.'

'That's a very harsh thing to say.'

'It's true all the same.'

'You have a poor opinion of men.'

'They like their own way,' Kirren said, 'and they always make sure that they get it.'

'Aren't women the same?'

'I've never had my own way in my life.'

'Perhaps you haven't gone the right way about it.'

'If you are trying to tell me that I need to be sweet and pretty and soft and admire everything men say or do – '

'I'm saying nothing of the kind.'

'What *are* you saying?' Kirren asked.

'Well, we seem to have strayed from the subject, rather, but in the beginning I was trying to ask you if you had thought deeply enough about this marriage proposition – '

'The marriage, as agreed between us, will suit me very well,' Kirren said. 'My father's been nagging at me for years to find myself a husband and I am sick of hearing it. By marrying you I shall get some peace. But his idea is a good one all round. It means you get the farm in the end, but without taking it away from me, and if you can really make it pay – '

'That I promise and swear to do.'

'Then I shall be well satisfied.'

'You seem very sure.'

'Yes. I am.' She looked at him with unsmiling gaze. 'If you can be sure, why can't I?'

There was no further argument after that; the matter was settled once and for all; and it only remained to see the vicar and arrange for the marriage to take place at the earliest possible date. And Jim, his last lingering doubts removed, felt free to give his mind to the farm.

Chapter Seven

It was a strange thing after living at Peele all these years, looking across the valley at Godsakes, to find himself now living at Godsakes, looking across the valley at Peele. It induced a queer feeling of dislocation in him, of dislocation, as though the sun itself were at fault for rising in the wrong part of the sky. Sometimes, in the fields at Godsakes, he would look up from his work and be stricken with a sense of confusion, because the tilt of the land was wrong and seemed to rear itself up at him, catching him unawares. But this confusion was purely instinctive, induced by sheer physical habit. He never for one single instant forgot where he was or why he was there.

The work at Godsakes was a challenge to him. His whole being rose to it, embracing it as a kind of crusade. His blood raced in response to it and he felt himself filled with the strength of three men. His mind was forever occupied with schemes, plans, calculations, ideas. While performing one task, he would be thinking over the next, so that no time was ever lost for want of knowing where to begin.

But although his mind was so full of schemes, it remained always cold and crystal clear. He knew what needed to be done and the best way of doing it. There was never any uncertainty. For one thing, he already knew the farm; had watched its downhill progress for the past fourteen years of his life; and had listened to John Sutton and Philip discussing what would have to be done to put Godsakes in order again when at last it came into their hands.

And here Jim's heart always gave a leap, because of the way things had fallen out; because Godsakes had come into *his* hands and the Suttons would never have it now – he would make quite certain of that. Philip had taken Jane from him and he in turn had taken Godsakes from them. There was immense satisfaction in this. It was a method of revenge that had a sense of rightness to it: a sense of fitness so complete that it tasted incredibly sweet on the tongue.

Whether it was right morally was, as he readily admitted, a matter of secondary importance to him, for he would have done it anyway without any compunction whatever. But there *was* a moral side to it and this added an extra dimension to the satisfaction he already felt. He had always had some sympathy for Morris Riddler in his struggles. The man had been treated badly by John Sutton, there was no doubt of that, and much of his life had been spoilt by it. Now Jim had given him the weapons with which to fight back and win. The two of them worked to the same end, the satisfaction of one magnified by that of the other.

'There's justice in this,' Riddler would say. 'I could almost believe in the goodness of God for sending you over to us.'

Not that they were always in agreement. Far from it, in fact. There were endless arguments between them, especially in the early days: arguments over the horses Jim bought; the implements, the new machines; and arguments over the new farm stock: the cows, the sheep, the pigs, the fowls.

'Why Shorthorns?' Riddler asked. 'What's wrong with Old Gloucesters, I'd like to know? And what do we want with so many sheep? The place is swarming with them already.'

'This farm needs the sheep,' Jim said. 'Especially on the lighter lands. They'll tread the soil and make it compact and their dung will put new heart into it. As for the cows, well, Shorthorns are more adaptable and milk better than Old Gloucesters do, and their milk makes better butter and cheese.'

'Well, if you say so, of course! It is your money, after all. I suppose you can spend it how you like.'

'Yes,' Jim said, 'and so I shall.'

'Even waste it,' Riddler said, 'paying it all out in wages!'

This was a sore point with him because Jim had engaged an

extra man, thus making three in all, and was paying them eight shillings a week.

'You can't expect good work if you don't pay for it,' Jim said, 'and six shillings is not enough.'

'You won't get good work out of Lovell and Smith. They don't know the meaning of the word.'

'I know well enough how they've played you up. I've seen the way they slack in your fields. But Townsend is a first class man. Abelard recommended him. And as he will get eight shillings a week, Smith and Lovell will get it, too. And if they don't earn it they'll be dismissed.'

'Have you told them that?'

'Yes,' Jim said, 'and they will find I'm a man of my word.'

These were among the first changes Jim made on the farm, for he wanted to get as much land ploughed that autumn as time and the weather would allow. And so it was, on a warm misty morning in mid-September, that there were five teams at work in the fields at Godsakes, three ploughing the fifteen acres of old oat stubble behind the barn, and two ploughing the borecole ground between the barn and the hazel copse.

Jim had not ploughed for three years. It was good to take hold of the stilts again and to walk behind a team of horses that steamed in the early morning air; to feel the ploughshare cutting the ground and to see the furrow-slice heeling over, burying the stubble and weeds and the rough clumps of couch-grass.

Riddler worked in the same field as Jim, grumbling all the while at his plough, blaming his horses and swearing at them when they turned too sharply at the headland, yet ploughing nevertheless with a certain jaunty, swaggering gusto, because of the new life and hope that had suddenly come to the run-down farm.

'Three years since you ploughed, did you say? For me it's more like five or six!' he called across to Jim once when both, on reaching the headland together, paused to give their teams a rest.

'You've still got the knack of it, anyway.' And Jim looked back at Riddler's stetch, its furrows running clean and straight.

Riddler also turned and looked back. Then he spat into his hands.

'I'm glad I'm still good for something!' he said.

The weather that autumn was open and mild and the work of ploughing, rolling, and harrowing went ahead without hindrance until just a few days before Christmas. Riddler grumbled endlessly at the many cultivations Jim considered necessary for the cleaning of the land and he thought it the height of folly that Jim meant to plough up certain 'pastures' only to sow the ground with new grass. The pasture in question was actually a neglected arable field where couch-grass had been allowed to grow, with stubborn weeds such as thistles and docks and even clumps of thorn and briar.

'This may be pasture to you,' Jim said. 'Myself, I would call it something else. Look at those sheep grazing there. They only graze one tenth of the field – the rest of it is unwholesome to them. Even the grass they do eat isn't nearly good enough for them – it will keep them alive but that's about all. I intend to sow proper leys, with the best seed-mixtures I can buy, containing clover and lucerne, and I'll sow forty pounds of seed to the acre to be sure of getting a good, close pile. And then I hope we shall have some pastures that are really worthy of the name.'

'Yes, if we're not both dead by then!'

Grass was just grass to Riddler and he would stare in astonishment when Jim pointed out the various species, giving their scientific names and describing their respective virtues. *Poas* and *festucas* were nothing to him and although he listened to Jim's 'lectures' it was only to pour scorn on them.

'Cocksfoot and cowgrass! That's all I know in the way of names. The rest is all flummery to me!'

It was the same with the artificial fertilizers Jim had bought.

'Guano?' he said, sniffing the sacks. 'All the way from Peru? Seems a bit far-fetched to me! And as for this bone-manure of yours, I don't see what we want with it. I've never used it in my life.'

'Are you holding yourself up as the best of examples?' Jim asked. 'Because if you are I would like to point out –'

'All right, all right, don't rub it in! I know I'm a failure!' Riddler said. 'You're the one that's running things now. I don't have any say any more. My only business these days is to stand with my mouth wide open in wonderment, watching you run my farm for me.'

But although he argued at every turn and was always making sarcastic remarks, Riddler's desire for Jim to succeed overrode everything else, even his jealousy and pride.

'I'd stand on my head if you told me to, if it meant doing good to the farm,' he said, 'and I damn well mean that, every word.'

'I don't want you to stand on your head, I want you to stand on your own two feet.'

'Hah! And what about my corns? Am I to put guano on them?'

'Yes, if you want them to grow,' Jim said.

Riddler went off with a loud guffaw and, passing Kirren in the yard, he said: 'One thing about this husband of yours! – At least we get a few laughs since he came!'

And as the fine autumn progressed and more and more land came under the plough, changing acres of grey scrub grass to the clean brown-ribbed pattern of ridge and furrow, Riddler's spirits expanded and soared.

'I hope John Sutton is watching this!' he said one day, jerking his head towards Peele. 'I hope he can see what's happening here. See what we're doing, you and me.'

Jim, forking field-rubbish onto a fire, paused and looked across the valley at Peele. The big square house, very white in the sunlight, against its dark background of trees, stood without any sign of life, but out on the land there was plenty of activity, especially in the arable fields, where the winter corn was being sown.

'He can see it all right,' he said quietly. 'He has no choice but to see what we do.'

'Well, that's the whole idea, isn't it? To show them what stuff you're made of, eh, and let that wife of Philip Sutton's see that she married the wrong man?'

Jim, in silence, turned back to his work, forking up the couch-grass and weeds that had been raked and harrowed out of the ground and placing them on the slow-burning fire.

'Well?' Riddler said, provokingly. 'Can you deny that's what you want?'

'I understand from Abelard that Philip and Jane are still away.'

'On their honeymoon?'

'Yes. What else?'

'Seems they must be enjoying it, staying away so long as this. How long is it? Five weeks or six?'

'I haven't been keeping count,' Jim said.

Riddler, so often forced to give in to Jim over the management of the farm, could always get his own back by taunting him in this way, and he took a malicious delight in it. Philip and Jane had been married on the second Sunday in October, a week after Jim's marriage to Kirren, and the young couple, according to gossip, were spending their honeymoon abroad, travelling in France and Italy.

'France and Italy!' Riddler would say. 'Now you could never have given her that. Not on a farm-bailiff's wages, eh? Not unless you had been prepared to spend all your savings doing so.'

Towards the end of November the young couple returned home and a week or so afterwards three large covered vans were seen driving up to Peele.

'Paintings and statues and sculptures and such,' old Abelard told Jim when they met down at the brook one day, 'and something my sister calls a spinette, that they've brought back with them from Italy.'

Whatever happened at Peele these days was soon known at Godsakes, and if some of the tales were exaggerated, obviously others were not, for the changes being wrought there, now that the house had a new mistress, could be seen and heard plainly enough. There were often parties in the evenings, when fine carriages came to the door and the whole house was a blaze of lights, and sometimes, when the wind was right, the sound of music could be heard across the valley at Godsakes.

'No wonder that girl jilted you,' Riddler would say, shaking his head. 'She wanted a lot more out of life than you could've given her, didn't she, eh?'

'Yes, it would seem so,' Jim said.

In between those times when the fallow lands were being cleaned by repeated cultivations, Jim and Riddler and the other men were busy cutting and laying the hedges, and day after day great fires of brash blazed and crackled in the fields, sending their thick grey smoke rolling out over the valley. The hedges were hawthorn, hazel, and ash, and because they were so badly overgrown, much stout timber was cut from them. This was trimmed, cut into lengths, and tied in bundles of such a size that each of the men employed on the farm could carry one home on his back when he chose. And the rest of the timber, stacked in the yard, was enough to feed the farmhouse fires for at least six months.

Jim also engaged a warrener to trap the rabbits infesting the farm and during the first month or so more than two hundred rabbits were killed. These were the warrener's source of income but often, when his 'bag' was extra big, he would leave a couple of brace at the house, so that rabbit stew and rabbit pie appeared regularly at the table.

'Better than reisty bacon, eh?' Riddler would say, grinning at Jim, and to Kirren, more than once, he said: 'You're getting to be quite a good cook now that you've got a husband to feed. This rabbit pie is something like.'

'Give me good meat to cook,' Kirren said, 'and I will give you decent meals.'

Certainly the reisty bacon had proved too much for Jim and he had soon asked Kirren to bring home a joint of fresh meat every week from the butcher's in town.

'A pretty penny that must have cost!' Riddler said, when the first of these joints, a rib of beef, was brought smoking hot to the table. 'But that's what comes of being genteel – his viands have got to be paid for in cash before they're good enough for him!'

101

'It's his own money he's spending, remember.'

'As though I'm likely to forget!'

'Are you going to carve?' Kirren asked.

'No, not me!' Riddler said. 'Not at sixpence a pound, I'm not! He paid for it, he can carve.'

Kirren, in exasperation, picked up the great dish of meat and put it down in front of Jim.

'I'm sorry about my father,' she said. 'He's always had this childish side.'

'Childish be damned!' Riddler said. He poured himself a mug of ale.

Jim picked up the carving-knife, sharpened it on the whet-stone, and tested the blade with his thumb. Then he picked up the carving-fork and began carving the joint.

'Nice thick slices for me,' Riddler said, 'and plenty of fat off the outside.'

These joints of meat, as Jim knew, had to be brought home by Kirren, along with all the other provisions, which meant a six-mile walk in all, sometimes in pouring rain. She would go in to the Wednesday market, carrying a heavy load of produce, and return almost as heavily laden with the week's shopping. As this caused him some concern he would, in the early days, walk down to meet her at Abbot's Lyall and carry her baskets the last two miles home.

Kirren was astonished – she had never been helped before – and because she was unused to it, she was inclined to be ungracious.

'You're wasting good working-time, trailing out here like this. I can manage perfectly well. I always have done, up to now.'

Riddler was even more astonished. He was also amused.

'Kirrie, you've married a gentleman! How are you going to live up to that?'

'We shall see if he stays a gentleman when he's lived here with you for a year or two.'

'One thing we may be sure of at least – he won't make a lady out of *you*.'

'Nobody asked him to!' Kirren said.

'It's her own fault she has to go to the town,' Riddler said. 'We used to have the higgler here, buying her butter and eggs and such, but she turned against him and stopped him coming. But you don't need to fuss over her. She's a good strong girl. She can manage a couple of baskets all right.'

'Yes, I daresay,' Jim said. 'But I don't intend that she should for much longer. I'm going to buy her a pony and trap.'

'God Almighty!' Riddler said. 'We shall end up at auction after all if you go on spending at this rate.'

'I don't need a pony and trap,' Kirren said, frowning at Jim. 'I'd sooner you hung on to your money in case of unforeseen trouble ahead.'

'What I spend on a pony and trap will not break us, I promise you.'

The trap was bought at a farm sale: rather old and shabby, perhaps, with its dark blue panelwork blistered and crazed, but sound enough in all other respects; and with it a docile Welsh pony called Griff, said to be eight years old but in fact nearer ten, Jim judged.

'Pot-bellied brute, isn't he?' Riddler said critically.

'He won't be, though, when he's properly fed.'

'I hope he understands English,' said Kirren, offering the pony a lump of sugar, 'because I don't speak any Welsh.'

The pony ate the lump of sugar and nuzzled her apron in search of more. She gave him a second lump from her pocket, then stroked his bristly, mottled nose.

'He understands sugar, anyway,' she said, and turned with a little smile towards Jim, who was standing nearby, watching her.

Riddler was also watching her and because it was such a rare thing to see her smiling in this way, with a faint flush of colour in her cheeks, he could not allow it to go unremarked.

'Why, Kirrie, what a difference it makes to see you looking pleased with yourself. It's something I haven't seen for years.'

'No, well,' Kirren said, 'it isn't every day of the week that you get given a pony and trap.'

'Seems you're like all the rest of them, then, if a man's got to dip into his pocket before he can get a smile out of you.'

103

'I didn't have to dip very deep,' Jim said, 'for the whole turn-out, harness and all, only cost me four pounds.'

'Oh, is that all?' Riddler said, affecting a grandiloquent tone. 'And four pounds, as we all know, is nothing to a man like you!' Then, in his normal voice, he spoke to Kirren again. 'But I must say it's worth every penny to see you smiling like that. You should do it more often. You should, that's a fact.'

'What for?' she said. 'To please you men?'

'There, that's gratitude for you, by damn!'

'And why should I be grateful to you?'

'Because, if I hadn't found you a soft husband, he wouldn't have bought you a pony and trap.' Riddler, pleased with his own logic, turned and walked away from them, saying in a loud voice as he went: 'A pony and trap, by God! – just to take a few paltry eggs and a bit of butter to town every week. Seems the chap's got more money than sense!'

Kirren, blank-faced, watched him go. 'He doesn't seem to realize that oftentimes in the past the money I've earned from my "few paltry eggs" has kept us out of the County Court.'

'I daresay he does realize it, but it wouldn't be an easy thing to admit, for a man with his pride.'

'Pride!' Kirren said scornfully. 'And what has he got to be proud of, pray, when he came within inches of losing this farm and then was only saved by you?'

'Your father's a fighter,' Jim said. 'Not clever, not wise, I grant you that, but a stubborn fighter through and through. It's always been a wonder to me that he managed to hang on as long as he did.'

'It seems you admire him,' Kirren said.

'Is that so strange?' Jim asked.

'To me, yes, it is very strange. But then, I've lived with him all my life. I know him better than you ever can.'

'You so often speak of him like that, and yet you have stuck by him all these years.'

'What else could I have done? Left him here all alone to drink himself into the grave? Turned my back on the place, knowing the Suttons would filch it from him? This farm is my

104

home, such as it is, and I certainly wasn't going to let it go so long as I still had breath in me!'

'All of which goes to show that, whatever you may say about him, you're your father's daughter after all.'

'Am I indeed?'

'I would say so, yes.'

'Well, I can hardly be blamed for that!'

Kirren turned to the pony again and after a moment Jim spoke of the trap.

'Have you ever driven before?'

'No, never.'

'Then you'd better have some practice,' he said.

A little while later Kirren was driving round the farm and Jim, beside her in the trap, was giving such advice as was needed in making the awkward double turn that led past the linhay and down the pitch. As they drove down the steep rutted lane and out onto the open track they were watched from the Middle Field where Lovell and Smith were at work together digging out the lower ditch.

'I reckon they make a handsome couple, don't you, Bob?' said Nahum Smith, leaning on his trenching-spade.

'Handsome enough,' Lovell agreed.

'I must say it came as a winger to me when Miss Kirren upped and got married like that. Somehow I never thought she would. But she's done pretty well for herself, marrying a chap like Jim Lundy, even if she was second choice as they say.'

'It's the farm he's married, not the girl, and if she has done well for herself, so has he, seeing he'll get the whole lot in the end. He's a fly young chap, our new master, for sure, and knows which side his bread is buttered?'

'As long as he goes on paying me eight shillings a week, he can be as fly as he likes,' said Smith, 'and damned good luck to him all the way.'

Kirren, now that she had her trap, could drive in to town in comfort and was glad of it, for the quantity of produce she took with her was growing all the time. There were six cows milking at Godsakes these days and six more were due to calve at intervals between Christmas and May. She had butter and cheese to sell again now and as there was more poultry on the farm – geese and ducks as well as hens – she also had many more eggs, often two baskets full every week.

Riddler scorned using the trap and even in the worst weather rode in to town on his grey pony mare who, as he said to Jim, could be trusted to bring him safely home even when, 'as happened sometimes,' he had had a glass or two more than was wise. But Jim, if he had business in town, often drove in with Kirren, partly because it suited him to and partly because he somehow felt that he and she, being husband and wife, ought to be seen together sometimes.

He never spoke of this to her. For one thing the feeling was much too vague and, as he told himself, rather absurd. Everyone in the district knew that theirs was not a marriage of love; that it was a cold-blooded partnership entered into for practical reasons; and it was nothing to him or to her that people knew this much about them. Why, then, did he have this desire to be seen now and then in public with her? It was, he concluded after a while, because he wished the world to see that, cold-blooded partnership though it was, he and she were well satisfied with it.

One market day when they went in to town and were on the many-gated road between Abbot's Lyall and Marychurch, they had a brief meeting with Philip and Jane Sutton who, driving a smart four-in-hand, came up behind them at Cooper's Bridge. Jim had got down to open the gate so that Kirren could drive through and he was about to close it again when the four-in-hand came bowling along. He saw at once who was in it and held the gate open for them, giving a little formal nod as they slowed down, crossing the bridge, and passed within a few inches of him. Jane, who was closest, smiled at him, somewhat hesitantly at first, then with a sudden radiance, and as she passed she spoke to him.

'Thank you, Jim. That was very kind.'

Philip drove past without a glance, staring ahead, red-faced and tight-lipped, and his angry annoyance was made worse when Jane again turned her head to nod and say good morning to Kirren, who had drawn in onto the verge.

'Damn it, why do you speak to them, Jim Lundy especially? He only opened the gate for us because he wanted to annoy.'

'Then why give him the satisfaction of seeing that he had succeeded?' Jane said.

Jim returned to his place beside Kirren and they drove on along the road, both of them silent for a time, watching the carriage in front as it rapidly drew away from them. Then Kirren spoke.

'So that is the famous Jane Sutton? I've never seen her close-to before.'

'You certainly saw her close-to today. She stared at you hard enough as she passed.'

'She was probably wondering what sort of creature you had married.'

'Yes,' he said curtly, 'I daresay she was.'

His mind was still full of Jane's smile; full of the memories it had evoked; and dwelling on these memories brought a kind of painful pleasure very difficult to renounce. But with an effort he purged himself, bringing his thoughts back to the present; back to the girl sitting beside him; and, turning to look at her, he said:

'Sometimes I wonder that myself.'

'What sort of creature you've married?'

'Yes.'

'Surely you must know that by now, having lived with me these three months or more.'

'I know you as cook and housekeeper, yes. As dairywoman and rearer of hens; as an extra milker when called upon . . .'

'In other words,' Kirren said, 'you know me as an all-round drudge.'

'You certainly work very hard.'

'So do we all. We have no choice. We are slaves to the farm, all three of us, bound to it body and soul.'

'Do you resent that?' he asked.

Kirren, considering, gave a shrug. 'I used to, in the old days, when everything seemed so hopeless,' she said. 'When it

107

seemed as though we should lose the farm however hard we worked to keep it. But that's all changed now, since you came. It isn't hopeless any more and I don't mind hard work so long as I see some reward at the end of it.'

'What reward?' Jim asked.

'To keep the farm, of course,' she said, 'and get it running properly.'

'It that reward enough for you?'

'What more would I want? Do *you* want more?'

'It's different for me,' Jim said. 'Work is a man's whole life but women, from what I know of them, ask for something more than that.'

'What am I supposed to want? A house full of servants to order about? Statues and paintings from Italy? A spinette to play on in the evenings?'

'I hope you don't want those things because I shall never be able to give them to you.'

'You may rest easy,' Kirren said, 'for the sum total of my ambitions, for today at least, is to get a shilling a pound for my butter and eightpence a dozen for my eggs.'

Jim smiled. 'And what about the future?' he asked. 'There must be things you would like to have.'

'Yes, there are, but I look to my poultry to pay for them, and as I've gone without them for so long, I can easily wait a while longer yet.' She gave him a brief sideways glance and said: 'I am not like your Jane Sutton. I'm prepared to work for what I want.'

No, he thought, as they drove on, Kirren was not like Jane. Indeed the contrast between the two young women – the one he had loved and the one he had married – could not have been greater. And as always when he dwelt on this contrast between them it was with the same angry elation that he had felt at snatching Godsakes away from the Suttons. It seemed peculiarly right, somehow, that whereas Jane was fair and blue-eyed, with gentle manners and a bright, easy smile, Kirren should be dark-haired and dark-eyed, with a temper that, more often than not, moved between sullen reserve and a quick, dark, withering scorn.

Kirren's life, from the age of six, had been made up of

108

hardship in all its forms. It had toughened her and made her strong, physically and mentally, and now at the age of twenty-two she had no softness or gentleness; no charm of manner; no feminine grace.

Jim took grim pleasure in this because Jane possessed these qualities and he had been led astray by them. That would not happen again; not with the girl he called his wife; for he expected nothing from her and therefore could never be disappointed. And although they had made certain vows in church, strictly as a formality, in private the only vow they had made was to work together for the good of the farm. Nothing else mattered to them. Only Godsakes, first and last.

Sometimes when Jim was working down in the meadows he would pause and look up at the farm and note the improvements made so far. They could be seen plainly from there, the three ploughed fields that were still bare showing up a rich red-brown between other fields already sown, where the winter corn was like a green mist creeping softly over the soil, and the new leys, a darker green, were already growing thick and close. Even the old neglected grasslands, grazed in turn by cattle and sheep, looked a healthier colour now, and where the hedges had been cut, the fields looked very trim and neat: larger, more open, more full of light.

'Are you pleased with what you see?' Riddler asked once.

'Yes, I am well pleased,' Jim said.

'So am I,' Riddler said, and for once he spoke simply and quietly, looking up at Godsakes with a bright, steady, satisfied gaze.

But the changes Jim had made so far were only a beginning: the first moves in a programme of improvement worked out to the last rod, pole, or perch; and the implementation of his plans would, he thought, take five or six years. He kept careful notes of everything that was done on the farm and often on cold winter evenings, beside the fire with Riddler and Kirren, he would discuss his plans with them.

'In five or six years, if all goes well, every acre we possess will have been cleaned and put in good heart again, yielding the best quality crops, supporting the best quality stock. I hope to start work on the buildings soon – I've ordered timber and tiles for the roofs – and next year we'll need to extend the byre. I also intend to build new stalls for fattening steers in wintertime, modern stalls built on modern lines, and in time everything on the farm – the house, the buildings, the land itself – will be in tip-top order.'

'In other words,' Kirren said, 'you want to make it a place like Peele.'

'No! Like itself!' he said sharply. 'It must have been a good place once, and it will be again, I shall see to that.'

'We shall all see to it,' Riddler said. 'But go on with what you were saying. I like to hear these ideas of yours.'

'I mean to have every inch of land producing its maximum yield,' Jim said, 'but exactly what that yield may be only time will tell.'

'If you're talking about corn, I can tell you the maximum yield on this farm – twenty bushels of barley to the acre and fifteen or sixteen of wheat. Not very good, I know, but if you were to sow twice as much as you are, that'd make up for the low yield and with corn prices holding up so well we'd make a small fortune next harvest-time.'

'The corn we grow on this land will not fetch the prices you're thinking of. Not till fertility's been restored. And that will only come about if we stock the land to capacity. All of which means growing crops we can feed directly to the stock. Turnips, kale, vetches, rape, carrots and beans. . . kohl-rabi, perhaps. And dredge-corn fed to them in the sheaf.'

'At present you're *buying* feed for them.' 'I don't see any profit in that. There's plenty of grass here, if nothing else, until we get our own arables. And as for this notion of feeding the ewes –'

'Ewes should always be given extra, coming up to tupping time, just as they get extra again shortly before they are due to lamb.'

'Chopped up dainty and fed by hand?'

'Chopped up, certainly,' Jim agreed.

'And what about the tups themselves? Don't they deserve an extra feed? Spinach, perhaps, or asparagus? Something sweet and tasty like that?'

Just as Riddler jeered at Jim on the subject of artificial manures, calling him 'Old Potassium', so too did he jeer when Jim quoted from certain pamphlets published by The Royal Agricultural Society.

'You can't learn farming out of books!'

'I didn't, I learnt it on the land. But books are written by men, remember – men who have tried things out for themselves – and it's only common sense that we should be willing to learn from them.'

Riddler picked up a small book that Jim had left lying about.

'This isn't one of your famous pamphlets?'

'No, that's something different,' Jim said.

'Shall I learn to suck eggs from it?'

'If you can read Latin, yes.'

'Latin! Good God!' Riddler exclaimed, and, opening the little book, he stared at the printed page in disgust. 'Lawyers' language! The language of rogues! *Damnum absque injuria*! Is that what your damned book is about?'

'No, it's a poem about farming, written by a man called Virgil who lived and farmed in Italy about two thousand years ago.'

'Two thousand years? You're codding me!'

'No, I'm not, I promise you.'

'Read us a bit,' Riddler said, tossing the book across to him. 'In English, so's we understand.'

Jim found a suitable passage, studied it for a moment or two, and then rendered it aloud in English:

' "*There comes a time when the corn is blighted; when thistles spring up everywhere; when no crops grow but wild tares and wild oats, beggar-weed and spiky caltrops. You must, therefore, wage war on the weeds unceasingly; cut down the trees that darken your land; shout the birds away from your crops and, in the summer, pray for rain. Otherwise, though your neighbour's granary be full, you will have to shake the acorns from the oak to stay your own hunger.*" '

Jim, as he closed the book and put it away, found that both

111

Kirren and Riddler had been listening to him as he read, and that both were looking at him intently, Riddler lounging in his chair, Kirren sitting erect in hers, with her needlework idle in her lap. After a moment Riddler spoke.

'You chose well, didn't you, reading that bit to us?' he said. 'It might have been Godsakes he was writing about, except that we never came so low that we had to eat acorns to keep alive.'

'No, just reisty bacon, that's all.'

Riddler threw back his head and laughed. He enjoyed these exchanges he had with Jim. And, although he continued to mock, he was more than a little impressed by Jim's superior learning.

'Kirrie, you've not only married a gentleman but a Latin scholar into the bargain. What do you think of that, eh?'

Kirren, resuming her needlework, snipped off a new length of cotton.

'I must try not to let it go to my head.'

Chapter Eight

During the worst winter frosts, when all work on the land was stopped, Jim worked on the house instead, replacing tiles that had slid from the roof, repairing ill-fitting doors, and repainting the big kitchen, which was also their living-room. He then began work on the outbuildings, putting new roofs on the sheds, laying new cobblestone floors, and whitewashing all the interiors. With help from Riddler and the other men the most urgent work was done in three weeks, and by then the frosts had gone, making field-work possible again.

'The rest of the house will have to wait,' Jim said to Kirren. 'I'm afraid it may be a long time before we get everything put to rights.'

'It doesn't matter,' Kirren said. 'The farm must come first, I'm aware of that.'

At least now the kitchen was fresh and clean, with its ceiling and walls distempered white and its oak timbers stained dark brown, and Kirren, cheered and encouraged by this, was adding improvements of her own. She had made new curtains, for one thing, and these, of a thick baize-like material in a pattern of rusty reds and browns, gave the room a look of warmth. She was often buying new things now that the poultry money was hers to spend as she pleased, and gradually the big room was becoming more homely and comfortable. There was new brown-and-white china on the dresser now, and a new set of earthenware jugs, brown-glazed outside, pale yellow within, eight of them in different sizes, standing on a shelf of their own.

One day, having been in to town alone, she returned wearing a new dress of dark green worsted, ribbed in black, with a double cape of the same stuff, and a black beaver hat with a curled brim. It happened that as she drove into the yard, Riddler and Jim were standing there, and both men stopped talking to stare at her as she drew up. Riddler was deeply impressed by his daughter's new outfit and hurried forward to help her down, a thing he never did as a rule.

'Why, Kirrie, I hardly recognized you, all dressed up to the nines like that! I thought it was some fine lady or other coming to call on us out of the blue.' And as he helped her down from the trap, he looked her over from top to toe. 'Lord, I'm struck all of a heap,' he said. 'I'd no idea you had it in you to look so very handsome.'

Kirren, with a satirical glance, extricated her hand from his and turned to take something from the trap. It was a large rectangular parcel, bulkily wrapped in paper and sacking, and she handled it with great care.

'What've you got there?' Riddler asked.

'You'll see when we get indoors,' she said.

Jim now went to the trap and took out the two heavy baskets of shopping. Riddler touched him on the arm.

'What do you think of your wife's finery?'

'I think pretty much the same as you.'

'Would you say she looked stylish, now?'

'Yes, I would, most certainly. Stylish and elegant, I would say.'

'Do you know,' Riddler said, as they followed Kirren into the house, 'I never noticed until today what a fine handsome figure she'd got on her.'

'Hadn't you?'

'No, I had not, and I reckon it must be the cut of the skirts and the way they flare out from the waist like that.'

'Fine feathers,' Jim said.

'Right so,' Riddler agreed. 'Still, she must've caused quite a stir, going about the town like that, looking so stylish and elegant.'

Kirren, although she had coloured a little, bore their comments with composure, walking before them into the house, the bulky parcel clasped in her arms.

114

'Whatever stir I caused in the town was nothing to the stir I seem to be causing here at home.'

'Well, open your parcel, girl,' Riddler said, 'and let us see what it is you've bought.'

What Kirren had bought was a pendulum clock, old but in excellent working order, in a case of polished mahogany, and with an engraved brass face bearing the maker's name, John Smith, and the words *Tempus Fugit*.

'That's one bit of Latin I *do* know, and it speaks the truth,' Riddler said.

Jim hung the clock on the wall straight away. He wound up the heavy weights, set the brass pendulum swinging, and cautiously turned the single hand, waiting at every half-turn while the clock struck, then setting it to the correct hour.

'Nice to have a clock in the place again,' Riddler said approvingly. 'This room is beginning to look very nice, with all the bits and pieces you've bought. More cheerful, like. More homely and kind.'

'And not before time,' Kirren said.

'How much did you pay for the clock?'

'Why, what business is that of yours?'

'I was just thinking to myself that if ever we fall on hard times again, at least we'll have something worthwhile to sell when we need some ready cash, eh?'

Kirren's face flushed darkly. 'You will not sell that clock,' she said, speaking with angry emphasis, 'nor any of the other things in this room, because *I* bought them and they are *mine* and you had better remember that!'

'God Almighty!' Riddler said. 'Can't you take a joke, girl?'

'It is no joke to me,' Kirren said, 'that you've stripped the house bare over the years.'

'I couldn't help but sell those things! I needed the money to pay the bills!'

'And how much of it went on drink?'

'Dammit, I've had enough of this! I'll take myself off outside and make myself useful there, looking after *your* pony for you and putting *your* trap away in the shed!'

Riddler went out, slamming the door, and Kirren, her

temper not yet spent, began gathering up the sheets of brown wrapping-paper, smoothing them out and folding them with quick, angry movements of her hands. Jim turned towards the door but paused a moment and looked back at her.

'It was only a joke, after all. Surely you must know that.'

'Oh, I know it well enough,' Kirren said, putting the paper away in a drawer, 'but I've never cared for my father's jokes and I doubt if I shall learn to now.'

Anger was always close to the surface in all Kirren's dealings with her father and it was easy to see why. The man was so rough and insensitive; everything he did was clumsy, ill-judged, often to the point of brutishness.

One morning in early March a polecat got in among the poultry and the noise and commotion were such that Jim and Riddler, who were in the barn, ran out to the yard immediately, followed in a moment by Kirren herself, who came hurrying out of the house. The polecat, laying about him in murderous fashion, took fright when the two men shouted at him and quickly made off, leaving behind him, on the ground, the mangled remains of three pullets, one of which still shuddered and twitched.

Riddler, bawling at the top of his voice, threw a stone at the fleeing polecat and then, still cursing and swearing, picked up the three mangled pullets and ran with them to the pig-run, hurling them over to the pigs who gathered at once to gobble them up. As he came lumbering back again, wiping his hands on his corduroys, Kirren confronted him in a rage.

'Why did you do that?' she cried. 'One of those pullets wasn't properly dead!'

'Well, it will be by now!' Riddler said. 'The old sow has made sure of that.'

Kirren, with a little exclamation, walked quickly away from him. Her face, Jim saw, was stiff with disgust. Riddler stood scowling after her, but when he turned and met Jim's glance, it was with a certain sheepishness.

'Women!' he said defensively, as they walked back to the

116

barn together. 'The damned bird was torn to shreds. Its head was half hanging off! So what was I supposed to do? Get the doctor out to it?'

'You should have wrung its neck,' Jim said, 'quickly, in the proper way.'

'What difference does it make? Either way, it ends up dead!'

'Women are sensitive about such things.'

'Too damned sensitive if you ask me.'

'Would you have them be hard as nails?'

'Oh, Kirrie can be hard enough when she likes.'

'Yes, well, she's had a hard life.'

'And what about me?' Riddler said. 'Haven't I had a hard life, keeping from going under all these years?'

'Yes, but it's different for you,' Jim said. 'You're a man. You can choose what you do. And you chose to stay put and fight for your farm, although you knew it meant hardship and poverty and possible failure at the end. But Kirren's a girl. She had no choice. And there can't have been much joy in her life, slaving away here with you for the past sixteen years or so.'

'You're just talking flannel, boy. Of course us men decide what to do, and if wives and daughters are what they should be, they're grateful to us for doing it. As for the joy in Kirren's life, it's up to you to give her that, and the sooner you get around to it the better because then perhaps she'll have something to do besides making a damned fuss over two or three bloody fowls!'

Riddler strode into the barn, seized the handle of the turnip-cutter, and began turning it vigorously, resuming the work that had been interrupted by the commotion in the yard. Jim followed him into the barn and stood watching him as he worked.

'In answer to what you've just said to me I feel I really must point out –'

'God, what a meal men make of things when they've had a good schooling!' Riddler said.

'You know the terms of my marriage to Kirren. You should do, since it was all your idea. A business arrangement, nothing more. That was what we agreed between us.'

'Yes, yes!' Riddler said, grunting as he turned the machine. 'But that was all of six months ago. I thought you'd have seen some sense by now.'

'You mean you expected things to change?'

'Of course I expected things to change! You're a man, aren't you, not an oddmedod? Flesh and blood like the rest of us? The same needs as other men?' Riddler stopped working and stood erect, breathing loudly and heavily. 'You're not still hankering after that girl who went and married Philip Sutton, are you?'

'No. I am not. But there's still no question of any change in my relationship with Kirren.'

'Oh, you'll come round to it in the end, sooner or later, you mark my words. You wouldn't be human otherwise. A man needs a woman to be a proper wife to him. It's only natural and right. And as for Kirren, well, I know she's got queer ideas about marriage and men, but she'll get over that in time, especially if you manage her right. I'm as sure of that as I am of death. A fine healthy chap like you, and a girl like her, built as she is! You're bound to come to it in the end. But don't take too damned long over it. I want to see a few children running about on this farm before I go to join my own wife under the sod in the churchyard.'

Riddler now took up a shovel and began shovelling the cut turnips into a wheelbarrow. Jim watched him, half vexed, half amused.

'Have you ever spoken to Kirren about these ideas of yours?'

'Why? D'you think I should?'

'No, I do not,' Jim said. 'I think you should put it clean out of your mind, for nothing will ever come of it.'

Riddler, still shovelling, shot him a glance.

'Yes, well, we shall see,' he said.

Under the brisk March winds, which blew hard and cold along the valley, the land was drying out nicely, and Jim, preparing for his first batch of lambs, chose a field known as the Browse, which lay up behind the house and was sheltered from the north by a belt of trees. The fifty ewes now folded here were those he had brought with him from Peele. They were due to start lambing in a few days' time.

Jim had placed shallow troughs in this field and into them the ewes' extra feed, so much oilcake and so much pulped turnip, was carefully measured twice every day. He had set up three hurdle pens and had scattered plenty of straw in them and here and there about the field he had placed a number of straw bundles, each securely tied with twine, so that the ewes, and their lambs when they came, would have warm 'cooches' as Abelard called them, against which to shelter from wind and rain.

Riddler, as was only to be expected, viewed these preparations with amusement.

'What about warming-pans?' he asked.

But this would be the first crop of lambs to be born at Godsakes for many years and now that the time was drawing close he was struck with a kind of anxious excitement, as though he could scarcely believe in these lambs that Jim took so for granted and talked of in such a glib way.

'I was never keen on sheep myself, and I only ever kept a few, even in the old days. They seemed more trouble than they were worth and I never had the patience for fussing and fiddling over them. But you're a different case altogether. You've got the patience of Job himself. And it shows in your flock. They're just about as pretty a bunch as any you'd see in all Gloucestershire. I'm proud to have such sheep on my farm. I am, that's a fact.'

'I'm quite proud of them myself.'

Jim was beginning the work of clatting. He had a ewe between his knees and was trimming away the soiled wool from under the tail and around the udder.

'I'll help you with that if you like,' Riddler said.

'No, there's no need. I can manage all right.'

'Won't let me near your precious ewes, not with a pair of clippers, eh?'

'You admit you lack patience with them.'

'And what about when the lambs start to come? Will you let me help you then?'

'Well, I've got Billy Smith coming to help with the lambing. He's a good boy with sheep. He's got the makings of a good shepherd.'

'And I haven't, you mean to say?'

'I think you've left it a bit late.'

'Cheeky devil!' Riddler said.

This early lambing went well and was all over in three weeks. The fifty ewes produced sixty-four lambs and of these sixty-two were raised. One ewe died giving birth to twins and these were kept in a pen in the barn, where Kirren tended them during the day, giving them milk from a newly calved cow. The twin lambs were sickly and delicate; so small that when she fed them she held them easily under one arm, letting them suck in turn at the bottle, on which she had fixed a washleather teat.

Riddler was very well pleased with the results of this early lambing but he disapproved of Kirren's efforts to rear the two orphaned lambs.

'It's nothing but a waste of time, rearing lambs by hand,' he said. 'Even if they pull through, they never amount to anything much.'

'What would you have me do with them? Throw them to the pigs?' Kirren said.

'Christ Almighty!' Riddler said. 'Am I never going to be let to forget what I did with those damned fowls of yours?'

He went off, muttering, and ten minutes later was mounting his mare out in the yard. It was a Friday and he was going in to the town to draw money from the bank for paying the men's wages next day. As he rode across the yard Kirren came out of the barn and he shouted over his shoulder at her.

'If I bring you back three pullets in place of the three the polecat took, shall I get a bit of peace at last?'

'I don't want your pullets,' Kirren said.

'Well, you'll get them whether you like it or not, and be damned to you for a nagging bitch!'

He was gone all day and when he returned after dark he was very drunk. He rode right up to the back porch and hammered on the door with his fist and when Kirren, who was alone in the house, reluctantly went out to him, he leant forward in the

120

saddle and dropped a closed basket at her feet. As promised, he had brought her three pullets.

In leaning so far forward, however, he lost his balance and pitch-rolled head over heels to the ground, bringing his saddlebags down with him. A faint sound came from his lips, half chuckle, half groan, and he made some effort to scramble up. But the effort proved too much for him; he gave another feeble groan, rolled himself over onto his back, and lay stretched, out insensible.

It was not the first time that Kirren had had to take charge of the mare, removing saddle and bridle, cleaning her and feeding her and bedding her down for the night. Nor was it the first time that Riddler had slept out in the yard, with a folded sack under his head and a horse-blanket thrown over him. Kirren performed these rough ministrations almost without a second thought. She then went to the poultry yard and put the three pullets into a coop, scattering a little grain for them and putting water for them to drink. By the time she returned, Jim had come in from the sheep-fold and was standing over Riddler's body. He had a lantern in his hand.

'He's pretty far gone.'

'Yes,' Kirren said.

'You surely don't mean to leave him like this?'

'Yes, I do. He's used to it.'

'Lying out on these cobblestones, on a fresh night like this, when it may well rain?'

'It's never worried him in the past. If it had he would surely have taken care to see that it didn't happen again.'

'He's not often as drunk as this.'

'Often enough,' Kirren said.

She picked up her father's saddlebags, heavy with the bags of coin he had drawn from the bank that day, and went indoors. She slung the saddlebags into a cupboard. It was past nine o'clock and she began preparing for bed, making up the fire for the night by heaping wood-ashes over it, and filling the kettle on the hook.

While she was doing this, Jim came pushing in at the door, carrying her father's limp body head downwards over his shoulder. 'I'm taking him up to his bed,' he said.

He crossed the kitchen to the opposite door and went out into the hall; she heard his tread on the creaking stairs; then in the bedroom overhead. She reached up to the mantelpiece, took down her candle in its holder, and lit it at the oil-lamp at the table. She stood waiting for Jim to come down, and the moment he entered the room she said:

'Perhaps you think *I* should have carried him up to bed?'

'No, I do not. But I think you could have done something more than leave him lying out in the yard.'

'That was where he chose to fall.'

'You are very hard on him.'

'Yes, I daresay.'

'He is your father,' Jim said. 'Your own flesh and blood. Don't you care anything for him at all?'

'No, why should I?' Kirren said. 'He's never cared anything for me.'

'I don't know how you can say that.'

'I know him better than you do. I've lived with him all my life. He's never been able to forgive me because I pulled through the flu years ago and my brother did not.'

'I'm sure that's not true.'

'I heard him say it,' Kirren said. 'I was out there in the yard and my mother and father were in the barn. "Why did it have to be the boy that died?" That's what he said. I heard it plain.'

'Did he say that?' Jim was shocked. 'That was a terrible thing to say.'

'Terrible? Yes, perhaps. But it's only what I felt myself. That if we had had the power to choose I would far rather my father had died than my brother Eddy who was only twelve and was always so quiet and gentle and kind. But we cannot choose. We have to accept. And that's what my father couldn't do. Oh, I realize it's not his fault that he cares nothing for me, but it's not my fault, either, that I care nothing for him.'

'What you overheard him say – people do say cruel things in moments of stress, things they don't really mean at all. I can understand how you've felt all these years, after hearing him say that, but I think you should try to forgive him now, if only for your own sake. It's wrong to store up bitterness.'

'Yes, well,' Kirren said, 'you should know about that, shouldn't you?'

For a moment Jim was taken aback. He had not expected such a counterstroke.

'That is scarcely the same thing. And I wasn't talking about myself. I was talking about you.'

'Yes, it's always easier dwelling on other people's faults. It helps you to overlook your own. But what was it that brought you here if it wasn't bitterness against the Suttons? Why did you make up your mind to stop them getting their hands on this farm if it wasn't to have your revenge on them?'

Jim was silent, staring at her. What she said was perfectly true and there was no denying it. But it was not the whole truth and, try as he would when he answered her, he could not prevent some sense of pique from betraying itself in his tone.

'You choose to overlook the fact that part of my reason for coming here was to help your father keep the farm.'

'It was part of your reason, perhaps, but not the whole. But you don't have to justify yourself to me because your coming here was the best thing that ever happened to us and the reasons behind it don't matter one jot. What you are doing on this farm profits us all equally.'

'I'm glad you can find it in your heart to give me some credit at least for doing good.'

'Is credit so important to you?'

'I am only human, after all.'

'A moment ago you were lecturing me for my lack of daughterly tenderness towards my father out in the yard. But at least I covered him with a rug. Perhaps you will give me credit for that.'

'If I did lecture you, I have been repaid in full,' Jim said.

'It seems we are quits together then, so I'll take myself off to bed before we begin wrangling again.'

The atmosphere had eased between them. There was humour in the glance they exchanged. But afterwards, when she had gone and he stood for a while alone in the kitchen, he was filled with an irksome restlessness; a sense of something left unresolved.

*

At five o'clock the following morning he was out in the lambing-pen, attending to his ewes and lambs, and as he went to and fro, he found himself brooding more and more on what Kirren had said to him about his bitterness against the Suttons.

Why it should so vex his mind he could not at first understand. The events that had led to his leaving Peele had indeed caused great bitterness in him, and that bitterness had prompted him to avenge himself on the Suttons. Furthermore, as he had to admit, he still felt immense satisfaction at having taken Godsakes from them. It was so right in every way. There was justice in it, as Riddler said. And Jim felt the same fierce elation now that he had felt at the very beginning. So why, when the fruits of his revenge were still sweet and satisfying to him, should he feel irked by what Kirren had said?

Slowly he realized that it was because the element of revenge was no longer of prime importance. He had been at Godsakes more than six months now and during the latter part of that time he had scarcely thought of the Suttons at all. He had been too busy; too absorbed. And he now saw, with great clarity, that what he was doing at Godsakes had become more important to him than his original reason for doing it – important for its own sake; important because it was good in itself.

This realization gave him a jolt of pleasure; a feeling of wholeness; a sense of release. And as he deliberately let his thoughts dwell on the Suttons – on the treatment he had received at their hands; on the way he had vented his spite on them by snatching Godsakes from their grasp – his feelings became clearer still, his pleasure more and more profound. The satisfaction was still there – he knew he would feel that all his life – but the bitterness and spite were gone.

With this discovery fresh in his mind he returned to the house. It was now half past six and Kirren was laying the table ready for breakfast. Jim was glad to find her alone and he came to the point immediately, wanting to get it off his mind before Riddler came in from milking.

'I've been thinking over what you said, about my feeling bitter against the Suttons.'

Kirren stood looking at him in surprise.

'It seems to worry you,' she said.

'Yes, because it's not quite true.'

'You still want to make me believe that you only came here to help us out of pure Christian charity and goodness of heart?'

'No, I've never pretended that. I came here, as I said at the time, because I wanted to spite the Suttons. But what I am saying now is that I no longer feel the bitterness you charged me with last night.'

'You mean you've forgiven them?' Kirren said, with barely perceptible mockery.

'I don't think,' Jim said, 'that I would put it quite like that.'

'But you do perhaps regret what you've done and would now turn us out of the farm so that your old friends the Suttons can have it after all?'

'I can see you're determined to make fun of me instead of listening to what I say.'

'I am listening now. With all my ears.'

'Are you indeed?'

'Indeed, I am.'

There was a pause. She looked at him. But her assumption of earnestness did not deceive him for one moment. He knew it was not intended to.

'It isn't easy, talking to you, when you so plainly think me a hypocrite.'

'Does it matter what I think? I told you last night that you don't have to justify yourself to me, but it seems you are determined to do so.'

'No. I just want you to understand.'

'You want me to think well of you.'

'I didn't say that.'

'It's true all the same.'

'Very well, supposing it is? Am I so different from anyone else? Don't you want to be well thought of yourself?'

'By you, do you mean?'

'By anyone.'

'Being well thought of,' Kirren said, 'is something I've had to do without, whereas you, being a man, take it for granted as your right.'

'You think me conceited, then,' Jim said, 'and altogether too full of myself.'

'You are no worse than other men. You have at least got something to be conceited about. You do at least get things done.'

'I've been a lot luckier than some. Luckier than your father, for instance.'

'You are always defending him. I don't know why that should be, I'm sure, when he talks to you the way he does, jeering at everything you do, even when he knows you're right.'

'I try not to let that worry me because I understand how he feels. I know how I should feel, myself, if I were in his shoes and had a stranger coming in, telling me how to run my farm.'

'You are certainly very patient with him. More patient than he deserves.'

'Your father is rough and careless, I know, and you have suffered at his hands. But he minds about you, in his way. I'm absolutely sure of that.'

'In his way? Yes, perhaps.'

'You are all he's got left in the world – of his own flesh and blood, that is.'

'So he's reminded me many times, and therein lies my importance to him. I'm all there is left of the old stock and he is hoping to breed from me.'

'*What?*'

'Have I shocked you, speaking so plain?' Kirren's dark gaze was amused. There was mockery in her tone again. 'I'm sorry, but I've lived so long with my father, the language of the farmyard comes easy to me.'

'It's not the language,' Jim said. 'It's the fact that you seem to have known all along what was in your father's mind.'

'That is never difficult. His mind is like an open book. When he suggested a business marriage, he thought it would turn into something else. I could see that as clear as glass.'

'And I,' Jim said wryly, 'saw nothing at all.'

'But no doubt he's spoken about it since.'

'Yes, a few weeks ago. How did you know?'

'He was bound to speak of it sooner or later. And, you may as well be warned, he's bound to speak of it again.'

'You don't have to worry about it,' Jim said. 'You have nothing to fear from me.'

'I know that,' she said steadily.

'I told your father, in positive terms, that he was to put it out of his mind.'

'Good advice, so long as he takes it. But he won't, of course.' And after a short pause she said, 'You never really finished saying whatever it was you were trying to say when you first came in.'

'You wouldn't let me,' he said with a smile. 'You thought I was making heavy weather of it and you were probably quite right. But what I was trying to say was this − that what I felt about the Suttons doesn't matter any more. At least, not in the same way. What I am doing on this farm is more worthwhile than anything else I could ever have done with my life and that matters more to me than simply having my revenge. Or, to put it another way, the fact that I no longer hate the Suttons somehow makes my revenge complete.'

He went outside to wash at the pump, and Kirren, as she prepared the breakfast, heard him talking to her father in the yard. After a while Riddler came in. He stood at one side of the hearth, watching her as she swung out the hook and hung the frying-pan over the fire.

'Somebody put me to bed last night.'

'Yes, I know.'

'Seems I've got a better son-in-law than I have daughter,' he said.

'By that same token,' Kirren replied, 'I've got a better husband than I have father.'

'I don't see that that follows at all.'

'At least he doesn't come home drunk.'

'Did you bring my saddlebags in?'

'Yes, they're in the cupboard there.'

'And what about the fowls I brought you? Did you see after them?'

'I shut them up last night and this morning I let them out with the rest.'

'Don't I get any thanks for them?'

'I'll thank you when they begin to lay.'

'And when will that be?' Riddler asked.

'It will never be, I'm afraid.'

'Why, what the devil's wrong with them?'

'They are all cockerels,' Kirren said.

Chapter Nine

Soon the second and larger batch of ewes began lambing and again, because of the dry conditions, all went well. These hundred ewes produced a hundred and thirty lambs and of these a hundred and twenty-six were raised, so that the lamb harvest altogether numbered a hundred and eighty-eight, including the orphans fostered by Kirren.

By early May, too, the six heifers bought in the autumn had all calved successfully, and were milking well, which meant so much more work for Kirren that Willie Townsend's wife Prue came every day to help in the dairy. They were making a good deal of butter and cheese at Godsakes now and much of the surplus buttermilk went to fatten the barrow pigs which, penned on a new piece of land every few days or so, were clearing the ground of rough grass and weeds, as well as enriching it with their dung, ready for ploughing at the end of the year.

The farm was teeming with life these days. The old silent fields had been transformed and on all sides there was movement and noise. In the evenings, especially, the gentle clamour of the ewes and lambs constantly calling to one another was heard from one end of the farm to the other, and, indeed, all over the valley.

'I hope *they* can hear it,' Riddler would say, jerking his head towards Peele. 'I hope it damn well pleases them that that handsome flock of theirs, bleating away over there, has got company here to answer them back.'

The farm was so heavily stocked now that towards the end of May Jim was glad to be able to turn his flock out onto the hills, thus giving the home pastures a rest and a chance to grow a fresh green bite. And all through May and part of June, in those fields that had been ploughed and harrowed and cleaned and rolled, and harrowed again to a fine tilth, the teams went steadily to and fro, drilling in the turnip seed, the rape and the kale, the chickling vetches, the peas and beans and French sainfoin. One half of the old winter pig-ground was sown broadcast with rye and the other with 'seeds' and so soft and moist was the weather just then that both crops were greening the ground within a mere eight or nine days.

On a warm sunny day in late June, Jim brought his flock down from the hill; onto the meadowland by the brook, where the ewes were separated from the lambs and herded into a long pen that led steeply down to the edge of the washpool. The upper sluice had been opened wide, the lower one almost closed, and as soon as the ewes were all penned, Jim and his helper, Billy Smith, lowered themselves into the pool, into water that reached to their very armpits. Riddler, in the pen with the sheep, seized one in his great clumsy hands and swung it over into the pool, where Jim in turn took hold of it, dunking it three or four times in the water before sending it down to Billy, who guided it onto the stone-paved slip that led up through a gap in the bank and out onto the open meadow.

Each ewe, as she struggled up to the top of the slip, stood for an instant dazed and drooping, weighed down by the water in her wool; but then, as the greater part drained from her, she would give herself a double shake that sent a little glistening shower rippling out from each side of her body. Another quick, rippling shake; a rainbow of droplets in the sun; and the ewe would move out over the meadow, giving a querulous, high-pitched cry that soon brought her lamb, or lambs, running to her with an answering cry; butting her with such eagerness that she was lifted off her feet, working away, pump and suck, at her cold, clean, watery udder.

This sheep-washing pool in the Timmy Brook had been dammed and banked many years before – as long ago, some said, as when the Benedictine monks had lived and farmed in this quiet valley – but the sluice-gates had been put in only a few years before by John Sutton, who at that time, was the only farmer using the pool. Neither Jim nor Riddler, therefore, felt any great surprise when they looked up from their work to find that they were being watched from the other side of the brook by two men on horseback. One, Jim saw at a glance, was Philip Sutton, and the other, he could easily guess, was Dick Bowcott, who had taken his place as bailiff at Peele. They sat their horses, talking together, and some way behind them, under an oak tree, Abelard leant on his shepherding stick, his dogs lying peacefully at his feet.

'Aye, you can watch!' Riddler muttered, as he flung a ewe into the pool. 'And think what thoughts you damn well please!'

He and Jim and Billy Smith went on working without pause but after a while the man Bowcott, obviously acting on Philip's orders, rode across the meadow to the pool's edge.

'How long are you going to be? Our shepherd is waiting to use this pool.'

'It's a damned funny thing,' Riddler said, 'that you should want to use the pool just when we are using it.'

'From what I've been told,' Bowcott said, 'you haven't used this pool for years.'

'Well, we're using it now,' Riddler said, 'and your shepherd will just have to wait his turn.'

Bowcott, plainly disliking his errand, could find nothing more to say, and Philip Sutton, perceiving this, now rode to the edge of the pool, there to look down with angry contempt, first at Jim, in the water, then at Riddler, on the opposite bank.

'You Godsakes people have no business to be using this pool at all, seeing that we put these sluice-gates in without a penny piece from you.'

'Sluice-gates or no sluice-gates, it's all as one to me,' Riddler said. 'The rights of washing our sheep in this pool are written into the deeds of my farm, just the same as they are in yours, and if you think you can stop us using it, you're an even bigger fool than I thought.'

'*Your* farm, did I hear you say?' Philip, defeated in argument, hit back at Riddler with a sneer. 'All things considered it seems to me that the farm is more Lundy's than it is yours.'

Riddler looked at him evenly.

'At least it'll never be yours,' he said.

'As to that, we shall see!' Philip said. 'There's many a slip between cup and lip and you've got a long way to go yet before you've paid off that mortgage of yours.'

He and Bowcott rode away. Riddler stood looking down at Jim.

'I don't know which I hate most, John Sutton or his son.'

'Take no notice of Philip's threats. He'll never take the farm from us.'

'No, he won't,' Riddler said, 'because if there was any chance of it, I should damn well kill him first.'

The sheep washing was resumed, but after a while they paused again to let the dirty water out and refill the pool with clean. While this was going on old Abelard came and spoke to Jim.

'That there fuss of Mr Philip's – I didn't have no part of it.'

'I didn't think you had,' Jim said.

'That's all right, then,' Abelard said. 'Just thought I'd mention it, that's all.'

As soon as the washing and shearing of the sheep were done with, it was time for haymaking in the meadows, and as soon as the hay had been carted and stacked, it was time for the weaning of the lambs. The ewes were put into poor pasture so that their milk should slowly dry off and the lambs were put into a field as far from them as the farm would allow so that neither ewes nor lambs should be distressed by the other's cries.

At the end of July came the summer sheep sales at Dunton Payne and here Jim's lambs were sold, together with a number of draft ewes, for a total of four hundred pounds. Riddler was up on stilts at this. He could scarcely believe his ears. That sheep from his farm should fetch such a sum! But Jim was already well known at the many local sheep sales, and, as the auctioneer remarked, so was his stock.

'My Lundy's Cotswolds need no introduction here,

gentlemen, and the interesting circumstance that he now farms at Godsakes instead of Peele has not, as you can see for yourselves, occasioned any decline whatever in the quality of his flock.'

'Why the hell should it?' Riddler muttered, but he was pleased nevertheless by the auctioneer's remark, and later that day, as he and Jim rode home together, he said: 'It's a pity the Suttons weren't there today to see your lambs fetch four hundred pounds, because there's not much chance of our losing the farm so long as we can raise stock that fetch prices like that, eh?'

'Are you still frightened of losing the farm?'

Riddler shrugged. 'I was thinking of what Philip Sutton said down at the washpool a few weeks ago, that showed he's still hoping to see us fail.'

'Philip has always believed,' Jim said, 'that he has only to want something and it will surely come to pass.'

'Sometimes it does, doesn't it, as when he took your girl from you?'

'Yes, well, sometimes it does. But Godsakes is another matter. Philip will never take that from me.'

'She can't have been much of a mucher, that girl, judging by the way she treated you.' Riddler glanced at Jim's face. 'Seems to me you're a lot better off married to my Kirrie,' he said.

'In the circumstances, yes, I am.'

'Damn the circumstances,' Riddler said.

'They are of your making, remember.'

'I thought to have seen you unmake them by now.'

'So you said to me once before.'

'Dammit, what've you got in your veins? Beetroot juice instead of blood? Or is Kirrie so unattractive to you that you can't bear the thought of bedding her?'

'I have no intention of discussing Kirren with you in this manner, now or at any time in the future, and you may as well make up your mind to it.'

'Strait-laced devil, aren't you, by God?'

'If you say so, certainly.'

'You're a lot different from what I was at your age.'

'That I can easily believe.'

'D'you want to know what I think?'

'No,' Jim said.

'I think you'll come to it in the end.'

'That, too, you have said before. But if by any chance you are right – '

'Yes?' Riddler said, with a keen, bright glance.

' – you may safely leave the matter in the lap of the gods and spare me all further importunings.'

'I suppose that's a gentleman's way of telling me to shut my mouth?'

'On this one subject, yes,' Jim said.

'Be damned to you, then,' Riddler said, and then, after another few minutes' ride, as they came within sight of The Crown at Marsh End: 'You can buy me a pint of ale for that and I'll drink to these precious gods of yours.'

Long before the day came round for paying their half-yearly mortgage dues Riddler wanted to pay off an extra portion of the principal sum.

'If we were to pay in the four hundred pounds we got for our lambs, that'd reduce the loan by more than half, and then it shouldn't be all that long before we can pay off the rest and be rid of it once and for all.'

Jim, however, would not agree.

'That four hundred pounds – and it's not all profit, remember – must go back into the farm, otherwise it will never improve. For one thing, we've got to buy more stock. For another, I want to build special tanks for dipping the sheep against the scab. Then there are the new sheds we need for stall-feeding steers in wintertime. And by the time we've done all that – '

'I know, I know!' Riddler said. 'There'll be precious little left and I shall be just as I have been for years – still with that blasted mortgage tied like a millstone round my neck.'

'So long as the farm is doing well, the mortgage dues needn't

134

worry us. They amount to little more now than the rent you paid in the old days when you were just a tenant here. But if we let the farm go down again – '

'Yes, well, you're right, of course. I can see it all clearly enough. But somehow, so long as that mortgage is there, sucking the blood out of us, I can't really feel that the farm is mine. And sometimes I get the feeling that I shan't live long enough to see the damned thing paid off at last.'

'Oh, yes, you will,' Jim said. 'It's only another four years and four months. Surely you can live that long?'

Riddler glared.

'I'll damn well have to, won't I?' he said.

It was a good summer that year, the soft, moist, misty spring, which had given the crops such a good start, being followed by dry spells in June and July, which enabled the horse-hoe to be used, clearing the weeds from between the rows and keeping the soil well-worked. And the crops, for the most part, were flourishing. Swedish turnips, sown in May, were bulging nicely in the ground by late July and were covered in a good growth of green sappy 'tops'. The rye, which was mown early in August, before it had time to go to seed, was soon growing tall again and would without doubt give another worthwhile crop in late September. The rape and the kale were doing well; so were most of the pulse crops, especially the long-pod beans; and, most beautiful of all, in Riddler's eyes, the eighteen acres of dredge-corn, oats and barley growing together, were ripening splendidly in the sun.

This was the first successful corn crop grown at Godsakes for ten years and Riddler could not keep away from it. He would visit the two adjoining fields two or three times a day, trying to estimate the yield, weighing a handful of grain from one against a handful from the other, his optimistic calculations rising higher every day. No oats ever danced so merrily, no barley ever bowed so low, as the oats and barley at Godsakes that year, and when the day came to begin cutting, Riddler was the first man in the field, wielding his scythe with such strokes that the corn went down in front of him, h'ssh-h'ssh, h'ssh-h'ssh, as though laid low by a fierce rasping wind.

'Can't you keep up with me?' he roared, pausing once and looking back to where Jim and the other men worked together, in echelon, some little way behind.

'The question is, master,' said Willie Townsend, 'can you keep up with yourself?'

But although, indeed, as the morning progressed, Riddler was obliged to slacken his pace, he nevertheless worked in a fever all through that day, and the following days, until the last of the corn was cut.

'I may not be so clever as some, but at least I can use a scythe!' he said.

Behind the men, as they cut the corn, came the women and children, binding the sheaves. There was much chatter and laughter then, especially from Willie Townsend's wife, Prue, for she shared her husband's sense of fun and could make a joke out of anything. When the last sheaf was bound, Prue tied her red and white neckerchief round it, held it up for all to see, and finally placed it in Riddler's arms.

'There you are, master! There's the neck and my neckerchief round it. What'll you give me in return?'

Amidst a burst of applause from the watchers, loudest of all from Prue's own children, Riddler gave her a smacking kiss and pressed a coin into her hand. He then carried the 'neck' aloft and placed it on top of a nearby stook. A warm southeasterly wind was blowing slantways across the valley; the oatseeds dangled and danced in it and the red and white 'kerchief fluttered gaily, and all over the harvest field, the rows of stooks went marching away, in regular columns, up and down whichever way you turned and looked.

'One thing about it,' said Nahum Smith, looking across the valley at Peele, 'we shall get our harvest in before *them*.'

This was a sly joke on Smith's part, made at Riddler's expense, for against the eighteen acres of corn grown at Godsakes the acreage grown at Peele was immense. Field upon field of pale-ripening wheat, field upon field of bronze-ripening barley, glowed on the opposite slopes of the valley, and day after day, from morning to night, the reaping machines chackered and whirred, and swarms of dark figures were seen, moving busily to and fro, bent double, in the wake of the reaper, first in one cornfield, then in another. These swarming figures looked black, like ants, seen against the pallid corn, moving over the pallid stubble, and all day long like ants they toiled, under the fierce, blind-burning sun.

Riddler made no secret of the fact that he was jealous of the harvest at Peele. Corn at that time was the glory of England. It ripened, guinea-gold in the sun, and, on land such as that at Peele, which had been cultivated to a state of perfection, it meant golden guineas for those who grew it. Riddler, looking across the valley, would sometimes stand in a kind of trance, shaking his head now and then, as though not believing what he saw.

'Just look at it!' he would say. 'More and more corn every year! And prices, from what I hear, just as high as they've ever been!' And once, coming to Jim, he said: 'How many acres all in all do you think they're harvesting this year?'

'Counting Granger's,' Jim said, 'I would say a hundred and fifty of wheat and maybe a hundred or so of barley.'

'And what profit will they clear on that?'

'I would say upwards of three thousand pounds.'

'By God!' Riddler said, and made a sucking noise through his teeth. 'And all we've grown over here is a paltry eighteen acres of dredge corn for feeding to the stock!'

'You know as well as I do that we can't grow good quality corn on this farm until we've built up fertility and as fertility depends on stock – '

'Oh, spare me the lecture for once, will you?'

'Anyway, this is a smaller farm, and even in the long term, when fertility's been restored, it will always need to be managed by different methods from those at Peele, if we're to get the best out of it.'

'*Your* methods, needless to say!'

'That was what we agreed from the start.'

'Everlasting bloody sheep! That's your method, such as it is!'

'Sheep will be the making of this farm. They are already playing their part in founding our prosperity.'

'They'll never make us a fortune, though, will they, the way corn is doing for the Suttons?'

'I promised to make Godsakes pay. I didn't promise you miracles.'

'Didn't you?' Riddler said with a scowl. 'I should have thought the odd miracle was nothing to a man like you!'

Contemptible though their own harvest might be, compared with Peele's, Riddler could think of nothing else and when, in a few days' time, the corn was carted to the stackyard and built into two neat round stacks, his pleasure and pride in them knew no bounds. Not usually a tidy man, he fussed over these stacks for hours, and while Smith and Townsend were up above, thatching them, Riddler was busy down below, first patting the sheaf-ends in with a flat piece of wood and then, still not satisfied, trimming them with sheep-clipping shears until the stacks were neat all round.

As soon as the corn was gone from the fields, the sheep and the pigs were put in onto the stubbles, to feed on the fallen ears of grain and to dung the land ready for ploughing. The pigs, rooting about in the ground, cleaned it thoroughly of couch-grass and weeds and turned it over at the same time, and this too was pleasing to Riddler.

'There are nothing like pigs for turning over the land,' he said. 'They work it better than any plough.'

At the sheep sales towards the end of August, Jim bought fifty theaves to make up his flock and four new Cotswold rams, great sturdy beasts, three years old, with a rich golden bloom upon their wool.

'Pure-bred, every inch of them, and don't they know it!' Riddler said.

At the Missenham cattle sale soon afterwards Jim bought a four-year-old Shorthorn bull, a handsome blue roan, costing thirty pounds.

'I never thought to see the day when Godsakes would have its own bull, let alone a bull like him that's got a dash of blue blood in his veins.'

Riddler enjoyed attending the sales: the outing, the gossip, the company; but, more important than this, was the fact that he and Jim were there, not merely as spectators but as buyers bidding along with the best. After the bleak, empty years it was pure balm to him to hear the auctioneer bring down his hammer with the words, 'Sold to Messrs Riddler and Lundy of Godsakes Farm.' And if it happened that the Suttons were there, as they were at Missenham when the bull was bought, then Riddler's joy was complete.

John Sutton and his son, with their bailiff, Dick Bowcott, always ignored Riddler and Jim and carefully took no interest in any item for which Jim was bidding.

'It's a funny thing,' Riddler would say, 'but they don't seem to get the same pleasure from seeing us at the sales as I get from seeing them!'

He was always conscious of the Suttons. They had become an obsession with him. Whatever improvements were made at Godsakes, he knew that the Suttons were bound to see them, and his pleasure was doubled, even trebled, thereby. As more and more land came under the plough; as old crops were harvested, new ones sown; as cartloads of timber and quarried stone were delivered at Godsakes for building new sheds, he would jerk his thumb towards Peele and say: 'I hope the Suttons can see all this! See what we're doing, you and me!'

One morning at breakfast time when he made some remark about the Suttons, Kirren suddenly burst out at him, exasperated by his refrain.

'Can't we forget the Suttons?' she said. 'Can't we get on with living our lives and give their names a rest for a change?'

'It might be easy enough for you to forget the Suttons, my girl, but it's not for me. Oh dear me no! Not after what they did to me.'

'I have just as much reason to hate them as you. What they did to us years ago spoilt my life just as much as yours and helped my mother to an early grave. But we have nothing to

139

fear from them now and it seems to me only common sense – '

'Nothing to fear?' Riddler said. 'There will always be something to fear so long as this land has a mortgage on it and that'll be for a long while yet!'

He finished his breakfast and went out. Kirren was left alone with Jim.

'Is it right, what he says? Must we always live in fear so long as the mortgage hangs over us?'

'No, there's nothing to fear,' Jim said. 'Not so long as we pay our dues, and that will not be any problem, now that the farm is productive again.'

'Ought I to go more carefully, buying things for the house? The money I make on my poultry these days – '

'Whatever you make, that money is yours, and you may spend it as you please. And in case you are worried about the future, I have enough money put by to cover any calamities.'

He rose from the table and pushed in his chair. He stood for a moment looking at her. 'You do believe me?'

'Yes,' she said.

'And trust me?'

'Yes.'

'I hope you do. You've had too much worry over the years. I'd like to feel that I've changed all that. I'd like you to feel safe and secure. Of course there are bound to be hardships enough. We'll have our troubles, our setbacks, no doubt. But we'll keep the farm and we'll make it pay and neither the Suttons nor anyone else shall ever take it away from us.'

'It's a pity my father can't believe that.'

'He will come to believe it, given time.'

In mid September the green rye was mown. It was turned in the swath and 'made' like hay. The weather was very hot at that time and because there were thunderstorms in the offing, all hands were out in the field, setting the rye up into cocks. But the thunderstorms passed them by; the rye was carted and built into stacks; and all the time as the carting proceeded, the weather continued sunny and hot.

Kirren, who rarely wore a hat when working in the fields, had caught the sun. Her skin, always dusky, became deeply tanned, while her dark brown hair took a lighter hue, especially at her forehead and temples, where the loose curling strands were bleached golden fair. Riddler strongly disapproved of women exposing themselves to the sun. He viewed Kirren's tan with some distaste.

'Kirrie, my girl, you're too brown by half. Jim must think he has married a gipsy. You're as brown as a nutmeg. You should wear a hat.' And, turning towards Jim, he said: 'Just look at her, how brown she is! Can't you get her to wear a hat?'

'I'm not going to try,' Jim said. 'Kirren is a grown woman. She's her own mistress. She may do as she likes.'

'Huh!' Riddler muttered, turning away. 'It's a pity she's not *your* mistress!'

Jim had now been at Godsakes a year. Much had been done during that time. Much remained still to be done.

'You'll do it all right,' Riddler said, as they walked together over the farm one Sunday evening. 'You're young and you've got most of your life before you. How old are you now? Twenty-five? Yes, you're lucky, you've got time on your side. Though in certain respects I must say I wish you would show a bit more dispatch.' Receiving no response to this he suddenly burst out in a passion: 'Dammit, man, don't you want a son?'

Jim looked away over the fields. The question had caught him unawares. Yes, he would have liked a son. Every man wanted that. And when he had hoped to marry Jane, he had taken it for granted that he and she, living together in the old farmhouse at Peele, would have raised a healthy young family. But all his plans had gone astray and he had committed himself to a life in which love and the joys of fatherhood would never now have any part.

Riddler, easily guessing his thoughts, broke in on them in his rough, gruff way.

'It's no good dwelling on the past, you know, moping over what might have been. It's the future you've got to think about and you need to face up to it fair and square. Stand still a minute and look at this farm. When I'm dead it will be yours — you and Kirrie will carry it on — but what about when you and she come to die? What will happen to Godsakes then if you've got no sons to come after you? Who will you leave it to? Answer me that!'

'I can't answer it,' Jim said. 'But the future you are talking about is, I hope, a long way off and at present I have enough to do thinking of more immediate things.'

But although he dismissed the future in this way, reluctant to discuss it with Riddler, he found himself thinking about it all the same and often in the following days he was filled with a kind of restlessness. A strange kind of loneliness came over him, bringing back old memories; not only of Jane, who had jilted him, but of his uncle Albert, the drover, who had treated him brutally as a boy and had at last abandoned him, in a strange district, all alone, caring not what became of him. He felt sorry for himself, a feeling he had not known for years, and he took himself sternly to task for it, remembering that many good things had happened to him as well as bad. Still, the same thoughts and feelings persisted, touching him sometimes with melancholy, and he thought how very strange it was that he, who had never known a father, should be fated never to know a son.

Sometimes, as he worked in the fields, he would see Kirren in the distance, shooing hens from the barn, perhaps, or carrying skimmed milk to the pigs, and he would think to himself: 'That girl, that stranger, is my wife.' And the thought, framed in words like this, brought a sense of shock even now. A sense of amazement and disbelief. How, how, he asked himself, had he come to agree to such a marriage? And, for that matter, how had she?

She was not such a stranger now, of course, for he had lived in the same house with her for a whole year. In some respects he knew her well: he knew what her capabilities were; he knew something of her history; and he knew what to expect of her

142

when her patience was tried, her temper roused. But what of her innermost feelings and thoughts? Her hopes and dreams? Her woman's heart? Was she so hard as she chose to appear? So unfeminine, so self-complete? Could she really be so indifferent to all ideas of love as to close her heart and mind against it so utterly?

He himself had experienced love and, disappointed in his hopes, he had turned against it. But Kirren had rejected it altogether. She wanted no part of it. It was something she scorned. But was such a thing possible? It seemed to him quite absurd that a young girl, in her early twenties, should choose celibacy as resolutely as any nun.

And why, asked a quiet voice in his brain, should Kirren's rejection of love be any more absurd than his? There was no answer to this, he thought, but an answer presented itself all the same: Kirren's rejection of love was absurd because she was a woman. Women were made to love and be loved. That was a fundamental truth. Anyone would say the same. And then he laughed, deriding himself, recognizing that he had been guilty of blatant male hypocrisy. Because, of course, it was man who chose woman's rôle for her, and man made the rules to suit himself; and if Kirren, for reasons he could well understand, chose to reject the whole scheme, why should it matter to him? It was none of his business, he told himself. It had, by a series of chance happenings, worked to his profit and advantage.

Still, he could not help wondering about her, and sometimes he wished they could talk together, quietly, just the two of them, without Riddler chipping in with his sly, provoking remarks. There were few opportunities for this but one day when he was up on the hill looking, for a bunch of sheep that had broken out of the upper pasture, he came upon her quite by chance, picking blackberries in a sunny hollow.

At first she was unconscious of him and he stood for a while watching her as she rose on tiptoe, with arms upstretched, trying to reach a high bramble that arched out from the centre of the thicket. It afforded him a certain amusement to watch her thus, all unknown, observing the slender shape of her body stretched to its uttermost, strong and lithe, as she reached up to the arching bramble. But then his two dogs, Jess and Sam, went running down the slope to her, wagging their tails, and she turned to make a fuss of them, giving each a few blackberries from one of her baskets, which was half full. Jim too went down the slope and when he got close to her he reached up with his shepherd's long stick and hooked the high bramble down to her. With a little laugh she picked the fruit and he let the bramble spring back again.

'Why are the best blackberries always out of reach?' she asked.

'What's out of reach always seems the best, whether it is or not,' he said.

He hooked down another high bramble and watched her pick the fruit from it. 'You've come a long way in search of these.'

'Yes. The farm hedges are so well kept since you came that there aren't any blackberries in them now.'

'The farm hedges are not so well kept as they should be, however, otherwise I shouldn't be here looking for five run-away sheep. You haven't seen them by any chance?'

'No, not a sign,' Kirren said.

'Ah, well, never mind. I shall catch up with them in the end.'

Jim laid his stick on the grass and motioned the dogs to lie down beside it. Kirren watched in surprise as he picked up the second of her baskets and began picking blackberries.

'I warn you, if you are seen doing that, it will lead to talk,' she said.

'Why?'

'Because it is women's work, of course.'

'You do men's work often enough, helping us in the fields,' he said.

'That's different. It's expected of us. But men do not help their womenfolk with such trivial tasks as this.'

'Then it seems I am not as other men.'

'No, that's true, you're not,' she said.

'Knowing your opinion of men in general, I suppose I may take that as kindly meant?'

'Yes,' she said, 'I suppose you may.'

It was a perfect September day and the blackberries, warm in the sun, filled the air with the smell of their ripeness. For a while Jim and Kirren picked in silence, moving slowly away from each other, around the thicket of bramble and briar. In a grove of hawthorn trees nearby a flight of goldfinches twittered and whirred and high overhead a skylark sang. The two dogs lay on the grass, alert yet relaxed, moving only to snap at the flies. Jim came to a bramble bush that grew no higher than his chest. Kirren was on the other side.

'I'm glad to have met you up here like this,' he said. 'It gives us the chance of a quiet talk. I was thinking about you as I came up the hill and it suddenly occurred to me that we have now been married a year.'

'Not quite a year, surely?' she said.

'Well, all but a week or two, anyway.'

'All but three weeks, to be precise. But surely, in a marriage like ours, we shall not be keeping anniversaries?'

'No, hardly that,' Jim agreed. 'It's just that it seemed a good time to be taking stock of ourselves as it were.'

'I'm not sure what you mean by that.'

'I suppose,' he said, thinking it out, 'I am looking for some sort of assurance that you do not have any regrets.'

'Then you have that assurance,' Kirren said. 'Our marriage suits me very well.'

'You are quite sure?'

'Yes. Quite sure.'

There was a pause. She looked at him.

'Have you any regrets yourself?'

'No. None.'

'Yet something is troubling you, I think.'

'I wouldn't say I was troubled exactly, but I have been looking back over the past and . . . thinking rather too much, perhaps, about certain aspects of my life.'

'You mean you've been thinking about Jane Sutton?'

'Yes.'

'Do you still love her?'

'No,' he said. He thought for a while before speaking

145

again. 'Love, as I see it, is a two-way thing. It's a kind of bargain that one human being strikes with another – or fails to strike, as the case might be. If love is one-sided, it doesn't last long.'

'Doesn't it?' Kirren said.

'Well, in very rare cases it might, I suppose . . . where the object is exceptionally worthy. But Jane was amusing herself with me, without any regard for my feelings, and that is not a worthy thing. However, I know I'm not the only man to have suffered such a blow to his pride, and I don't intend to let it spoil my life. We can most of us get along perfectly well without love – if we are called upon to do so.'

'It doesn't seem to bring much happiness to those who are afflicted with it.'

'We are better without it, you would say?'

'I thought that was what you were saying.'

'Yes, well, perhaps it was.'

For a while they gave their whole attention to the business of picking the blackberries. Then Jim spoke again.

'Certainly there's a lot to be said in favour of a marriage like ours, based as it is on a practical footing instead of on sentimental ideas. It means we do not ask impossible things of each other, and that, in turn, means that neither of us can fall from grace. The very fact that we have been married a year without any serious disagreement speaks very well for the arrangement, I think. Indeed, the only person who isn't pleased is your father, whose idea it was.'

'Ah, yes, my father,' Kirren said.

'We are a great disappointment to him.'

'He will get over that in time.'

'I'm not sure that he will,' Jim said.

'Then he must just put up with it.'

'Unfortunately for me, your father's disappointment is not something he keeps to himself, as you already know.'

'Yes, and I'm sorry,' Kirren said, 'but what can I do about it?'

'Nothing whatever, I'm afraid.'
'I think you bear it very well.'
'I have no choice,' he said ruefully.

Chapter Ten

The warm sunny weather continued right up to Michaelmas Day and then came a sudden change. The last of the autumn ploughing was done in a searing north-easterly wind and the winter corn was no sooner sown than it was lightly covered with snow. The snow did not lie long because rain came and washed it away and the rest of the autumn was so wet as to stop all further work on the land.

The wet weeks were not wasted, however, for Jim and the men were hard at work building the new cattle stalls that would house the steers for fattening in winter. Jim was keen on this system, not only because of the profit that winter-fed beasts would bring, but because of the saving of manure. The stalls, open along the front and built round three sides of a square yard, were finished by the end of November and twenty-two steers were housed in them. Jim then turned his attention to the farmhouse, doing all those repairs that had been left over from the previous winter.

If anyone entered the front door at Godsakes — which, as in many a similar farmhouse, was in fact a rare event — and stood in the wide passageway, a door on the left led into the kitchen and a door on the right, under the staircase, led into the only other ground-floor room, which Riddler called the house-place and Kirren the parlour. There was no furniture in this room — it had all gone to pay Riddler's debts — and for years the place had only been used for storing sacks of grain and meal and a great variety of lumber. But it was a fine, spacious room, half as long again as the kitchen, with two double casements at the front, overlooking the valley, and two single casements at the back, looking towards Hogden Hill; and, at the far end of the room, a fire-place with a big open hearth.

The lumber and sacks of grain were removed, the dirt and cobwebs were swept away, and the whole room was scrubbed throughout. Jim then got to work; repaired the cracks and holes in the plaster; whitewashed the ceiling, between the beams, and distempered the walls a pale shell-pink. The timberwork was all oak, including the plank-and-batten door, and this he treated with linseed oil. The casements were metal and he painted them white.

Kirren, meantime, had been busy shopping. She had bought three rolls of thick fibre matting which, laid on the stone-flagged floor, felt warm and kindly under the feet; also a dark red Wilton rug which made a cheerful splash of colour in front of the hearth. She had bought some second-hand furniture, too, which Jim fetched home in an open cart: a dining-table of dark oak, with four ladder-back dining-chairs; three Windsor armchairs, with flat cushions on the seats and backs, for sitting in comfort at the fire-side; and a book-case to hold Jim's books and Riddler's collection of almanacs. There was also a large, handsome lamp, which held a quart of oil at a time, and had on it a round shade of rich amber-coloured glass engraved with a pattern of ivy leaves. Lastly there were some heavy curtains, old but with plenty of wear in them, of crimson and gold brocade. Kirren had to alter these to fit the windows at Godsakes and with the material that was left over she covered the cushions on the Windsor chairs.

'Oh, it's a fine handsome room right enough.' Riddler said, 'if only we had time to sit in it.'

But in less than a week it was Christmas, which fell on a Sunday that year, and Riddler, in the middle of the morning, looking in at the door intending to scoff, stood on the threshold and marvelled instead. For the room, with a great log fire in the hearth, with red-berried holly on the beams over-head and sweet-scented pine-branches over the door, with the table arrayed in a white linen cloth on which the silver cutlery and the smoothly polished pewter mugs reflected the red glow

149

of the fire, was a warm and welcoming place indeed to a man coming in from feeding the beasts on a winter morning, cold and raw.

'It does you credit, Kirrie,' he said, 'and I only wish your mother was here to see the place made so homely again.' He was much impressed by the cutlery – 'You must be making a pretty penny out of your poultry and eggs these days' – and by the three white linen napkins which lay, each in its horn ring, on the side-plates of brown-and-white cottage ware. 'I'd no idea you had it in you to be so genteel,' he said. 'I must go and spruce myself up before I'm fit for a room like this.' And later that day, after a dinner of roast goose, followed by a rich dark plum pudding, served with thick cream, he said: 'Kirrie, I reckon you've done us proud! I doubt if they've had a better Christmas dinner at Peele than the one you've given us today. You're as good a cook as your mother was and I can't speak better of you than that.'

He and Jim went to sit by the fire and when Kirren had gone from the room, leaving them to their hot spiced wine, he sat back in his armchair and looked around him appreciatively.

'It's good to see the old place coming back to life again. You and Kirrie between you have made it into a proper home. All it needs now to make it complete is a few children sitting here, gathered round the fire with us, and all of us playing "Robin's Alight".'

Jim remained stubbornly silent, staring into the heart of the fire, his mug of spiced wine between his hands. Riddler, watching him, gave a sigh.

'Ah, well!' he said, sadly. 'You can't stop an old man from dreaming his dreams.'

The parlour was used every Sunday after that. It became a regular thing and Riddler teased Kirren about it.

'You're getting ideas above your station, my girl. It comes of marrying a gentleman.'

The mockery was automatic. He was in fact well pleased with the improvements Kirren had made. And gradually certain changes were taking place in Riddler himself. He was now shaving regularly and was taking more trouble with his clothes. His boots and gaiters were well-polished, his breeches and jacket brushed clean, and he had bought himself a new hat. Jim and Kirren, although they noted the change in him, said nothing to Riddler himself, but Kirren mentioned it to Jim.

'My father's a different man these days. He's not so slovenly in his habits and he goes off to town now looking quite smart. He's easier to live with than he was. All of which is due to you, because of the way you've pulled up this farm. You've given him back his self-respect. He's able to hold up his head again.'

'Your father has always held up his head, even in the bad times, and so have you,' Jim said.

'You can't refuse,' Kirren said, 'to take the credit for saving the farm, because that would be too absurd.'

'There was a time when you seemed to think I was taking too much credit for it.'

'Did I say that?'

'Well, not in so many words, perhaps. But you had a few sharp things to say about my motives for doing it.'

'Your motives are neither here nor there. They've faded away into the past. It's what you've done that matters to us.'

'Yes, it's what matters to me as well.'

The new year came in cold and wet and although there was nothing surprising in this it was, as it turned out, setting the pattern for the rest of the year. Some ploughing was done in the upper fields, where the land was light and well-drained, but by the beginning of February the heavy unrelenting rain had turned the whole farm to mire. Down in the valley the Timmy Brook flooded the meadows for weeks on end. The little bridges were all submerged and when Kirren drove to town, she had to go round by Marychurch and cross the river at Lyall Bridge.

Even in the wet weather, there was always plenty of work to be done, for the dark winter days were all too short. Horses were taken to be reshod by the blacksmith at Angle Green; plough-coulters went for sharpening; traces went to be repaired; and while the horses were out of the way the stables were given an extra good clean and then white-washed. Every bit of harness was oiled; all tackle checked and repaired. Waggons were varnished; axles greased; every tool and implement cleaned and sharpened, as need be, or given a smart new coat of paint.

Still the rain came teeming down, keeping the men off the land, and still Jim found things for them to do. He set them to whitewash the inside of every outbuilding on the farm; all the sheds, both new and old; the pig-sties, the hen-coops, the privvies, the barns; and 'even the damned cart-shed!' Nahum Smith said in disgust.

'What are you complaining about?' Willie Townsend said to him. 'Would you sooner the master laid us off?'

The bad weather saw them into the spring. Even March brought little relief. There were a few dry days towards the middle of the month but then, just as the first batch of lambs were due, the rain descended yet again, cold and heavy, out of the north.

The lambing went badly from the start and although Jim took extra care, providing all the shelter he could and spreading the lambing-pens with straw, conditions were so wet and cold that many ewes, in giving birth, were too enfeebled to play their part.

'That's the trouble with sheep,' Riddler said. 'They give in too easy. They've got no spunk.'

He and Jim and Billy Smith were out at all hours, attending the ewes in their labour, rubbing life into weak, sickly lambs, and doing their best to get them to suck. But in spite of their vigilance and care, a great many lambs were lost to them, and, in time, a number of ewes.

'Ah, what's the use!' Riddler said, as he added yet another corpse to the heap already awaiting disposal. 'That's how it's always been on this farm – just when you think things are picking up, whoosh, and you get slammed down again!'

Kirren, bringing hot food and drink to the men at work in the lambing-field, saw the heap of small dead bodies lying sodden and limp in the rain and turned away, sick at heart.

'How many have you lost?' she asked, as Jim came to take the food-basket from her.

'So far, more than half,' he said.

His expression was bleak, reflecting her own, and he looked at her with tired eyes. But it was not the work that had tired him; it was because so much of the work had been in vain; and Kirren, who knew what his flock meant to him, was stricken anew.

'So many?'

'Yes, it's bad.'

She looked past him, up the field. A number of ewes, who had yet to lamb, were grazing in a desultory way, each with its rump to the rain and the wind. A few others, with their lambs, lay in the shelter of the hurdle pens.'

'What about the live lambs? Will they pull through all right?' she asked.

'I hope so, but it's hard to tell. A lot depends on the weather. If it goes on like this – ' He gave a shrug. ' – we are bound to lose a few more, I'm afraid.'

Riddler came stamping down the field, impatient for his dinner. He had heard Jim's last words and was cocking an eyebrow at the sky.

'It's no good looking for a change,' he said. 'This rain will be with us till Kingdom Come. I can feel it in my chines.'

It was the cold and the wet together that did so much damage in the flock. A ewe could easily stand the cold if only she had a dry resting-place and a lamb, too, could withstand the cold so long as its birth-coat had a chance to dry out. But the rain that spring showed no mercy and ewes that would not lie down on wet ground remained on their feet until exhausted. Thus, many lambs were stillborn, and others, already weak at birth, died within a matter of hours.

Still, miraculously, there were survivors, most of them lambs from older ewes. Some of these, both the lambs and the ewes, needed special care and attention, and every available shelter had been brought into use as a nursery. There were also a few orphan lambs, kept in a separate pen in the barn, and it was Kirren who looked after these, warming cow's milk for them, carefully diluted with water, and giving it to them from a bottle. She also tended two ewes suffering from garget, washing their inflamed udders, rubbing them gently, morning and evening, with the elder ointment Jim gave her, and, when their condition improved, persuading them to accept their lambs.

Kirren was good with animals. Nothing was too much trouble for her. And Jim, noting her gentleness whenever she handled a sickly lamb or patiently coaxed an awkward ewe, was not only grateful for her help but deeply moved by her concern for the dumb creatures in her care. The animals themselves sensed her concern. They responded to her and trusted her.

And with all this, Kirren still managed her other duties. The dairywork was done just the same; the chickens were fed and the eggs collected; the housework, the washing, the weekly baking, were all accomplished as usual. If the men were out at night with the flock, she would come to them with hot food and drink, and every morning, by five o'clock, she was sure to be in the kitchen, with a good fire burning on the hearth, the kettle steaming over it, and breakfast already on the go.

'When do you sleep?' Jim asked her once.

'When do *you*?' Kirren retorted.

One cold dark morning when she was giving her father his breakfast Jim came into the kitchen and, partially opening the front of his jacket, showed her a new-born lamb which he was carrying inside; a lamb so incredibly small that Kirren had to peer close before she could believe it was there and make out its shape in the jacket's folds.

'Oh, how tiny!' she exclaimed, and put out a hand gingerly, to touch its coat of tight, close curls. 'I've never seen such a tiny lamb. It's scarcely so big my two hands.'

154

'He's one of twins,' Jim said. 'The ewe has turned her back on him – she hasn't enough milk for both – and he's only just barely alive. Can you look after him indoors? Keep him warm here by the fire?'

'Yes, of course,' Kirren said.

'Have you got something to put him in? A basket or a box of some kind?'

'Yes, I'll find something suitable. Just leave it to me.'

All her attention was on the lamb; she wanted to take possession of it; and Jim, opening his jacket further, eased it carefully into her hands. It was the merest morsel of life, all head and ears, its frail body nothing at all, its long legs limp and knobbly, like the legs of a rag doll. Kirren folded it into her arms and it nestled against her, wearily, its head lying against her bosom, moving against her, seeking her warmth, until, with a little sudden thrust, it buried its nose under her armpit and rested there, with a little sigh.

'It must be the smallest lamb ever born,' she said. 'I've never seen such a scrap of a thing.'

'He's spoiling your pinafore,' Jim said. 'I haven't properly cleaned him up.'

'Never mind. I'll see to that. The most important thing right now is to get some warm milk into him.'

'I'll leave it to you, then.'

'Yes,' she said.

Riddler, at the table, now put in a word.

'It's nothing but a waste of time raising lambs by hand. A waste of time and energy.'

'He always says that,' Kirren said. 'He said it last year, just the same.'

'He's probably right about this one,' Jim said. 'I doubt very much if it will survive.'

'Then why have you brought him in to me?'

'I wanted him to have his chance.'

'Exactly,' she said. 'And so he shall. His little heart seems strong enough. I can feel it thumping against my hand.'

'Well, we shall see,' Jim said, and touched the lamb's head

where it lay on her breast, still with its muzzle tucked under her arm. 'If you can manage to pull him through the first two or three days or so . . .'

'I can but try.'

'Yes, that's right.'

Jim turned towards the door. Kirren, frowning, called to him:

'Aren't you staying to have your breakfast?'

'No, I've got to get back to the pens. I'll be in again in about half an hour.'

Riddler, sitting longer than usual over his own breakfast, watched with a mixture of interest and scorn as Kirren dealt with the new-born lamb, bedding it down in a shallow box lined with hay, and placing it to one side of the hearth, where it received the warmth of the fire but not its full heat. She then took some diluted warm milk, stirred a little sugar into it, and added two or three drops of brandy. She put the milk into a drinking-bottle and, crouching down beside the lamb, tried to insert the washleather teat between its tightly clamped little jaws.

This proving difficult, she smeared a few drops of the milk on his lips, gently persevering with him until at last he opened his mouth and licked the milk with his small pink tongue. When she had done this a number of times she was able to persuade the lamb to receive the teat into his mouth. There was a faint snuffling noise as he blew through nostrils not quite clean; a gulping sound as his small throat worked; and, in a moment, quietness, meaning that he had learnt to suck. And at the end of the small wrinkled body lying curled in the box, a wispy tail waggled and twitched.

Riddler had finished his breakfast now. He rose from the table and pushed in his chair.

'It's high time you had a lamb of your own,' he said in a deep-throated growl, and pushed past her to get at his coat which was hanging up by the fire-place.

Kirren was silent, feeding the lamb, and he stood looking down at her broodingly.

'Did you hear what I said?'

'Yes, I heard.'

'Then why in God's name don't you answer me?'

'Because I don't know what answer to make.'

'I just don't understand you at all. You're a woman, aren't you? You're not made of stone? And you've been married a good eighteen months – '

'Married at your instigation, remember, as a business arrangement, nothing more. That's what you said to us at the time, and that's what we agreed, Jim and me.'

'But damn it, girl, you must have known that I had something more in mind?'

He humped himself into his coat and fastened the buttons up to the neck. The lamb had had enough for its first drink and Kirren now rose to her feet, the half-empty bottle in her hands.

'Yes, I knew what was in your mind, but it wasn't in my mind, nor in Jim's.'

'More fool you, then!' Riddler said. 'And more fool him too!'

'More fool all three of us, it would seem.'

'I thought I'd done pretty well by you, finding you a husband like Jim, a well-set-up chap, healthy and strong, with something more about him than most.'

Kirren became silent again, turning away from him to the hearth, where she placed the lamb's bottle on a ledge to keep warm. Then she removed her soiled pinafore, laid it over the back of a chair, and went to take a clean one from the drawer of the dresser. She put the loop over her neck and tied the strings behind her back. She smoothed the pinafore down in front.

'Hell and damnation!' Riddler exclaimed. 'Jim is a handsome enough chap, I'd have thought! Not that looks account for much, but you women set some store by them, especially when it's a case of a chap with clean blue eyes and light fairish hair. Of course, he's got his faults, I allow. He's a pig-headed devil for a start – '

'Hark who's talking!' Kirren said.

' – and inclined to think he's always right.'

'So he is, more often than not.'

'Seems you think pretty well of him, then?'

'I have good reason to think well of him and so have you. Without him we should have lost the farm.'

'I'm not talking about the farm.'

'I know quite well what you're talking about.'

'He thinks well of you, anyway. That much is obvious, I should have thought. You can tell by the way he talks to you, the way he treats you so civilly, the way he helps you at every turn.'

'Jim treats me the way he does because he happens to be that kind of man.'

'A gentleman?'

'Yes, I suppose.

'I reckon there's more to it than that.'

'Do you indeed?'

'Yes, I do. He feels something for you, Kirrie, I'm sure. Why, the way he looks at you sometimes – '

'And what way is that?' Kirren asked, in a tone crisp-edged with disbelief.

'It's the way any man will look at a girl, so long as she's comely enough and young, with a face and figure worth looking at. And with Jim being the man he is – '

'You are making all this up. I have never seen Jim looking at me in the way you are talking about.

'You wouldn't, would you?' Riddler said. 'He would take good care of that, just in case of offending you and making you think he'd gone back on his word. He knows your views on marriage and men. You made all that pretty clear from the start. And a young man of Jim's sort needs some sign from a girl, first, before he'll come out in the open with her. Remember, he's been hurt once before and he wouldn't want to risk that again, so it's up to you to encourage him and let him know you've changed your mind.'

'I didn't say I'd changed my mind.'

'Then what the hell did you say?' Riddler exclaimed, his patience giving way to wrath.

'Nothing that's worth saying again.'

'I wish I could get you to talk sense sometimes.'

'And I wish *you* would leave me alone!'

Abruptly Kirren moved to the table and began clearing the used breakfast things. Riddler, swearing under his breath, took his hat from the fire-place and jammed it down hard on his head.

'Stupid cat of a girl!' he muttered, and went out, slamming the door.

Within a few hours of being brought indoors the lamb, thoroughly warmed through, had left his bed beside the fire and was exploring the kitchen, tottering over the flagged floor on legs that were apt to crumple beneath him. In a matter of three or four days, although his legs might still let him down, he was able to right himself without help, and would follow Kirren constantly while she went about her chores. Fed every three hours or so, both night and day, he was slowly picking up strength, beginning to take a lively interest in everything that happened around him.

'He's doing nicely,' Jim said. 'You've pulled him through the most difficult time. He's got it in him to thrive from now on.'

'Do you think he will?'

'I'm sure of it.'

The early lambing came to an end, having lasted fifteen days. Of the seventy-six lambs born, only forty-two had survived, and, with the weather still bad, a few more of these might still be lost. Of the sixty ewes that had lambed, five had died, and another eight or nine would be useless for future breeding.

Anyway, it was over now, until the second lambing began. Life for Jim would be less of a strain during the next three or four weeks and he would be able to sleep in his bed instead of snatching an hour at a time in a chair by the kitchen fire.

On the morning that the last two ewes had lambed he came into the kitchen at ten o'clock when Riddler had just ridden off to town and Kirren was about to begin her baking. As she moved between cupboard and table, setting out the things she would need, the hand-reared lamb, now eight days old, followed her faithfully to and fro, still uncertain on his legs but showing a bright, adventurous spirit.

When Jim entered the room the lamb scampered towards him, put up his chin to be fondled and scratched, and then, with a little flouncing movement, went lolloping over to his bed. It was occupied by a tortoiseshell cat expecting kittens who had that morning chosen it as a suitable place for her lying-in. As the playful lamb nuzzled her body she put out a slow, lazy paw, pushing against his woolly face with just a slight suggestion of claws, sharp enough to make him draw back. He veered away from her to the hearth and peered into a shallow basket wherein crouched a bedraggled hen, surrounded by a number of chicks, all of which Kirren had rescued from a flooded ditch in the home pasture.

'It seems there's almost as much livestock indoors as there is out,' Jim remarked. He stood looking down at the lamb. 'I've come to take this chap off your hands. I think I've got a mother for him. It's the ewe I've just left – her lamb was stillborn.'

'Can I come and watch?'

'Yes, of course.'

They went together through the rain, across the yard to the open barn, Kirren with a shawl over her head, the lamb tucked under her arm. Inside the barn, as they crossed the threshold, there was a gentle surge of warmth; a warmth that was all the more grateful because of the greyness of the day and the steadily falling rain outside. The warm barn smelt of the penned sheep and lambs; of the straw trampled under their feet; of the sweet dry hay in the hay-bags that Jim had tied all along the pens.

He led the way across the barn to a pen against the far wall. In it stood the bereaved ewe, she who had lost her lamb that morning, her rump still red from the birth, her attitude listless and dejected. But her tight-stretched udder was full of milk and she would make a good mother to the hand-reared lamb if she could be persuaded to accept it.

Jim opened the front hurdle a few inches and entered the pen. From his pocket he took a bottle containing balsam of aniseed. He got astride the ewe from behind, uncorked the bottle with his teeth, and poured some of the strong-smelling oil into the palm of his left hand. Kirren, still carrying the lamb, stood close by watching him and he gave her the bottle to hold. He then began rubbing the oil under the ewe's chin and jaws and all round the outer rims of her nostrils. Protesting a little, she tried to break free, but Jim had her wedged between his legs, one hand firmly under her chin, and in less than two minutes the job was done. Satisfied, he let her go, and she moved away, shaking herself. He took the lamb from Kirren's arms, rubbed a little of the oil on its hindquarters, and set it down on the floor of the pen.

Although the pen was quite small, the ewe did not see the lamb at first. She was busy moving her head up and down as though trying to escape the smell of the all-pervasive aniseed. But when the lamb began to bleat she turned and stared at it in surprise, in a way that seemed quite clearly to say: 'Where did you come from? You are not mine. Or, are you?' Jim put the lamb closer to her and she leant towards it, suspiciously, sniffing it without touching it.

But her sense of smell was badly impaired by the strong smell of aniseed; the lamb had the same smell, anyway; and in another moment or two, although still plainly mystified, she had stepped forward and was sniffing him close, working her way down his back with a nibbling movement of her lips, as though she meant to eat his wool. The lamb gave a short, rippling shudder and turned towards her, butting her side. Jim guided him to a teat and as soon as he began to suck, so his tail began to twirl. The ewe, looking over her shoulder at him, viewed the movement indulgently, giving a little whickering cry, quietly, deep in her throat. Ewe and lamb, so it seemed, were very well pleased with one another.

Jim emerged from the pen and lifted the hurdle back into place. Kirren gave him the bottle of oil and he put the cork back into it. They stood together watching the lamb as it pumped with increasing confidence at the ewe's swollen milk-bag.

'He'll be all right now,' Jim said. 'They both will. She's a good mother, this one. He'll do well with her, though they'll both need coddling for a while, just like all the others here.'

Kirren nodded, looking around at the many couples housed in the rows of hurdle pens. She turned back to Jim.

'So that's the last of the lambing for now?'

'Yes, praise be.'

'You've lost a great many.'

'Yes, it's been bad. I've never had a lambing like it before. Smith and Townsend are out there now, burying the last of the carcasses. Still, it could have been worse, I suppose . . .'

'Could it?' she said, doubtfully.

'No, you're right, it couldn't,' he said. 'And I hope to God by the time the next batch start coming the weather will have improved a bit.'

'It must, surely,' Kirren said.

'Yes, surely,' Jim agreed.

They turned and walked to the open doorway and stood looking out at the rain. It was falling coldly and heavily; white shafts of it slanting down to splinter and splash on the cobbled ground.

'It doesn't look like improving yet.'

'No, it's setting in for the day. Your father will have had a wet ride to town and he'll have a wetter one coming back. There's a good two feet of water covering the bridges over the brook and Smith says it's rising steadily. If your father's got any sense he'll come straight home when he's finished his business at the bank.'

'But he hasn't got any sense at all. You should know

that by now. He'll stay chatting all day to the market folk, taking a glass with this one and that one, and won't be home until after dark. But his mare usually brings him safe home. *She* has some sense, even if he has not.'

'You are hard on him,' Jim said with a smile.

'You think so, I know,' Kirren said.

'He may behave foolishly now and then, but he's not really a fool, you know.'

'Isn't he?'

'No, he is not. He sees certain things clearly enough, and he has his own rough wisdom sometimes, if only you could recognize it.'

'One thing at least I recognize – he has a loyal ally in you.'

'I'd like to think,' Jim said, 'that I am an ally to both of you.'

Kirren glanced at him; then away.

'Yes, and so you are, of course.'

Staring out at the cold white rain, she seemed for a while to be lost in thought. But she knew that Jim was watching her and as the silence lengthened between them he saw that she was not quite composed. There was a frown between her eyes that suggested some disturbance of mind, and in the dark eyes themselves there was a look of uncertainty. He was about to speak to her when suddenly she turned away, going back into the barn to look at the newly fostered ewe and lamb. The lamb had stopped sucking now and was standing in front of the ewe, bracing himself, splay-legged, as she licked his body with vigorous tongue. Kirren returned to Jim at the door.

'I needn't concern myself about *him*, that much is obvious,' she said. 'He's doing very well indeed.'

'You will be glad, I daresay, to have your kitchen to yourself.'

'Yes, and I must get back to it.'

'Back to your baking?'

'Yes, that's right.'

'Not to mention your hen and her chicks.'

'And Tibby, the tortoiseshell cat,' Kirren said, 'who may well have had her kittens by now.'

'Your kitchen is a menagerie.'

'And you said I'd have it to myself!'

She looked out again at the teeming rain and pulled her shawl up over her head.

'I really must go,' she said.

'But it's raining harder than ever,' Jim said. 'I think you ought to wait a while.'

'No, it's all right.' She flashed him a glance. 'I must make a dash for it.'

He watched her run across the yard and vanish in a flurry of rain between the dairy and the byre.

Chapter Eleven

The rain continued all day, growing heavier all the time. By afternoon it was falling in torrents and the whole farm was awash. Special drains had to be dug to carry the water out of the yards. Ditches everywhere were overflowing, flooding the fields, and every track was a running stream. There was no great gale of wind; no thunderstorm; just a solid downpour of rain, hour after hour, all day long.

Jim, coming into the house at two o'clock, ate his food as fast as he could and went out again into the rain. The greater part of his flock, ninety-five ewes in lamb, were standing over their hooves in water in the home pasture and so chilled and dispirited were they that this new onslaught of rain seemed likely to pound them into the ground.

'We're taking them up to the pinewood,' Jim said. 'It's the only place that's not flooded and at least they'll have some shelter there.'

By four o'clock it was almost dark. The men passing the kitchen window on their way to the milking-shed were dim, dark shapes in the gloom, hooded and hunched against the rain. When Kirren went out to the dairy, a distance of only a few yards, her thick cloak was soaked through and her boots filled with water instantly. And before she could attend to her duties there, dealing with the milk as it was brought in, she was obliged to light the lantern hanging from the beam overhead.

Down in the bottom of the valley the Timmy Brook had broken its banks and was spreading out over the meadows in a great sweeping tide. By half past six the meadows were covered and the water was still rising steadily. Jim went down with Townsend and Smith to take a closer look at it and found that the swirling floodwater had covered the lower part of the track. It was completely dark now and Jim carried a lantern. The three men stood at the gate and watched the floodwater rising until it covered the lower bar.

'It's worse than I've ever known it, even in winter,' Smith said, 'and I've been on this farm more than twenty years.'

'What about the master?' Townsend asked. 'Will he come round by Lyall Bridge?'

'I don't know, but I doubt it,' Jim said. 'He doesn't take much account of the floods and he won't know just how much worse it is until he actually gets to the brook.'

'The bridges will all be under three or four feet of water at least,' Smith said, 'and judging by the way it's swirling here I'd say the current is pretty fast.'

'Yes, I think you're right,' Jim said. 'I'm going down to watch for him.'

'Shall we come with you, master?' Smith asked.

'I reckon we ought to,' Townsend said.

Jim looked at the two men, huddled in the pouring rain, their faces only just discernible in the glimmering lantern light. They had been working fourteen hours and for most of that time had been soaked to the skin.

'No, there's no need for you to come. Get off to your homes, both of you, and get yourselves into dry clothes. But there is something you can do – you can call at the house on your way and tell Mrs Lundy where I am. Tell her I've gone down to the brook to wait for the master coming home.'

'We'll tell her, sure enough,' Townsend said. 'But are you sure you should go down alone? I don't much like the look of these floods and what with it being so tarnal dark –'

'Don't worry,' Jim said. 'I shall take care, be sure of that.'

Leaving the main farm track he went splashing across the meadow through water that reached half way up his shins. The rain, although it had slackened a little, was still quite heavy enough to make the night as black as pitch and in the darkness the great meadow, so familiar by day, seemed like a never-ending waste, full of unremembered dips where thick mud sucked at his boots and made progress difficult. His lantern was no help in finding the way; it merely lit a small patch of rain and cast a will o' the wisp reflection on the floodwater swirling about his feet; but a sense of direction was strong in him and he trusted himself to it with confidence. Still, he knew that caution was needed and when he felt the water deepen, he began moving very slowly, testing the ground with each foot before putting his weight on it. At last a willow tree loomed up at him and he knew he had reached the bank of the brook.

For a while he stood perfectly still, listening to the noise of the brook, waiting for instinct to guide him in choosing which direction to take. When he had made up his mind, he reached up to the willow tree and broke off a long, slender branch, and, proceeding with even greater caution, began moving rightwards along the bank, prodding the brook in search of the bridge. The floodwater now reached to his knees, eddying round him with a force that told him how swift the main current must be, and he felt the force of the main current, too, in the way it dragged at the willow branch.

He knew well enough which of the bridges Riddler was in the habit of using but finding it on such a night was a different matter altogether. He feared that his instinct had played him false – that he should after all have gone left on reaching the brook – and he was thinking of turning back when he felt the ground begin to dip and the water to rise above his knees and knew that he had arrived at the place where the bank sloped down to the bridge. And, prodding the bridge with his willow branch, he judged that the water covering it was, as Nahum Smith had predicted, between three and four feet deep.

There was no telling when Riddler would come. It could be any moment now or it could be as late as nine o'clock. Jim had to resign himself to the possibility of a long wait. And what if, after all, Riddler came home the safest way, by the bridge at King's Lyall? 'Then,' Jim said to himself, 'I shall have had my long wait for nothing.' But he felt sure in his bones that Riddler would come by his usual route, and so it proved, for when he had waited perhaps an hour he heard the sound of hoofbeats coming across the flooded meadow on the far side of the brook.

Standing on the bank above the bridge, he raised his lantern shoulder-high, swinging it gently to and fro, at the same time putting one hand to his mouth and calling out in a great voice that would carry above the noise of the rain:

'Morris! Is that you?'

Riddler, approaching the flooded bank, heard Jim's voice calling to him and was able to pick out the light of the lantern glimmering on the other side. He had no need to draw rein, for the mare, who had already slowed to a walk, now stopped of her own accord, gently pawing the flooded ground where it began sloping down to the bridge.

'Of course it's me!' Riddler called back. 'Who else would it be, for God's sake?'

'I don't think you ought to cross here – it's too dangerous,' Jim called. 'I think you should go round by Lyall Bridge.'

'Don't tell me what to do!' Riddler bawled. 'I've crossed this brook in flood before and never got myself drowned yet, so stand aside, out of my way, otherwise you might get hurt!'

This answer was only what Jim had expected and he knew it was no use arguing.

'Very well!' he shouted back. 'But keep a close rein as you come across. The current is running very fast.'

'My mare's not afraid of the water, current or no current, by damn!'

Sure enough, encouraged by Riddler, the mare picked her way through the deepening water and down onto the narrow bridge, and, with the flowing brook now up to her belly, began very gingerly to cross. When she was half way across, however, a floating log, coming down on the floods, struck her a sharp blow in the ribs. The sudden shock and the force of the blow, together with the swift rush of current, caused her to side-step on the bridge. She gave a high-pitched whinny of fear and the next instant was in the water, hindquarters plunging with a great hollow *plump*, forefeet wildly pawing and splashing.

Riddler, half drowned, held her up, first swearing at her and calling her names, then speaking reassuringly to her.

'Come on, old girl, you must swim for it now. That's the idea! You're doing fine. Don't let the current bother you. It's only a yard or two more to the bank.'

168

Jim, although he could see almost nothing, knew from the noise what had happened and guessed what had caused the mare's plunge. Knowing, too, that the swift current was carrying her downstream, he made his way along the bank, coming, after twenty paces or so, to the place where mare and man struggled together in the brook.

'Morris?' he called. 'Are you all right?' And Riddler shouted in response: 'Damn you! Get out of the way! We're coming up just there!'

The mare had great difficulty in mounting the steep, slippery bank but, urged on by Riddler's shouts, she humped herself up and over at last in three gallant, heart-bursting heaves. But as she made the final heave, bringing her shuddering hindquarters up over the edge of the bank, Riddler was thrown out of the saddle. He fell heavily sideways, head and shoulders striking the ground, while one foot remained in its stirrup, twisted round in such a way that, try as he might, he could not pull it free; and as the mare cantered away, he was dragged along the ground beside her, bump and splash, all through the mud and the floodwater. Once, for a few brief seconds only, he managed to raise his head and shoulders, reaching up with outstretched arms, trying to catch at the flying reins.

'Whoa, you fool, would you kill me?' he roared. Then he fell back again into the mud.

The mare passed close enough to Jim for him to sense what was happening and as she went cantering over the meadow he heard Riddler's desperate shout. He too shouted for her to stop but she ran on, frightened and confused, making instinctively for the gate that led onto the main farm track. And Jim, splashing across the meadow, followed her blindly through the darkness.

The closed gate brought her to a stop and she was waiting, all in a tremble, when he at last caught up with her. Soothing her as best he could, he hung his lantern on the saddlehook, and gathered up the trailing reins. Riddler was unconscious now, but still alive. Jim freed his foot from the twisted stirrup and heaved him up into the saddle, holding him there with one hand while he opened the gate with the other. Still speaking quietly to the mare, he led her up the track to the farm.

Kirren, hearing him in the yard, came out at once to the porch door. She watched him carry her father in.

'What happened?' she asked.

'The mare missed her footing on the bridge. She had to swim across the brook. Your father was thrown out of the saddle but his foot got caught up in the stirrup and he's been dragged right across the meadows.'

'Is he hurt badly?'

'I don't know. But he's unconscious and he's soaked to the skin. We must dry him and get him into bed. Can you put a warmer in?'

'Yes,' and she went to see to it.

Jim laid Riddler down on the mat in front of the fire and stripped off his clothes. He gave him a good hard towelling and rubbed warm brandy into him; into his chest, his stomach, his back; even into his legs and feet. Then he wrapped him round in a warm woollen blanket round him and carried him upstairs to his bed. Kirren had put a hot brick into it, wrapped in a thick flannel cloth, and this he pushed down to Riddler's feet. She had placed a lighted candle nearby and now she was lighting a fire in the grate. The sticks, kept warm in the kitchen hearth, made a good fire immediately, and she put on a number of small dry logs. She rose from her knees and came to the bed.

Riddler lay flat on his back, with the bedclothes drawn up to his chin, his queer, crooked face as pallid as yeast, his damp hair streaked down over his skull, and a slow trickle of watery blood oozing from a cut above one eye. His breathing was so shallow and quiet that he seemed not to breathe at all. Kirren touched his face with her hand. She looked at Jim.

'How bad is he, do you think?'

'I don't know.'

'He feels very cold.'

'Yes, and his pulse is very weak.' Jim turned towards the door. 'I'm going to fetch Dr Hoad,' he said.

Kirren followed him down the stairs and into the kitchen.

'You're not going to cross the brook, I hope?'

'Yes, I am.'

'After what's happened to father tonight? Are you out of your mind?'

'It won't happen to me,' Jim said.

'How can you be sure of that?'

'Your father'd been drinking. I have not. I'll come to no harm, I promise you.'

'Why not go round by the main bridge at Lyall?'

'Because, as you well know, it will add an hour or more to the journey.'

'I see no point in saving an hour if you end up drowned,' Kirren said. 'I know what the brook is like in flood. And what about the mare, anyway? Will she cross again after such a fright?'

'I hope she will. Indeed, she must. It wouldn't be any good taking Griff. He's not used to it. She is.'

'I wish you would not go,' Kirren said. 'You may not have been drinking, it's true, but when did you last have a good night's sleep? Oh, I know you've slept in that chair, a couple of hours at a time, perhaps. But when did you last sleep in your bed? You've been out with your flock at all hours this week – ' She broke off, looking at him, and her eyes were suddenly very dark. 'You're just about tired unto death,' she said.

There was a little silence between them, full of feeling, full of thought, and they looked at each other across the room.

'I'm not so tired as all that . . . and I think it's important to get the doctor as soon as I can.'

'Dr Hoad won't cross the brook. He'll come the safe way like a sensible man and if you had half an ounce of his sense – ' Once again she broke off, giving vent to a short, sharp sigh. 'Oh, it's no use talking!' she said. 'I'm wasting my breath, I can see that! Go and get yourself drowned in the brook if that's what you've set your heart on doing!'

She turned away from him, angrily, but he caught her arm in a firm grip and drew her round to face him again.

'I shan't drown,' he said quietly. 'I care too much about my life to run any risk of losing it.' And, stooping, he kissed her on the mouth.

171

A quick glance between them and he was gone and Kirren, left staring at the door, heard him riding out of the yard. For a moment she stood, listening, her thoughts going with him through the night. Then, with a faint flush of warmth in her cheeks, she turned and went out to the hall and up the stairs to her father's room, to sit with him and watch over him until such time as Jim returned.

When the mare, as Jim expected, jibbed at crossing the brook again, he dismounted and led the way, stepping down onto the bridge, into water that reached above his waist, and coaxing her to follow him. She gave a snicker of protest at first, but responded trustingly enough to the firm pull of his hand on her bridle, and they crossed safely to the other side.

It was turned half past eight by the time he reached the doctor's house and rain was still falling steadily.

'Can't it wait until morning?' the doctor asked irritably.

'No, it can't,' Jim said.

'Oh, very well, very well, I'll come! But not with you, mind, across your damned brook. I'm too old for such pranks as that. I shall come round by the bridge at Lyall.'

Jim returned home the way he had come, again without any misadventure, and Kirren, having been listening for him, came to her father's bedroom window, peering down through the rainy darkness and raising a hand to him as he rode past on his way to the stables.

When he went into the kitchen, after attending to the mare, Kirren was busy at the hearth, preparing hot food for him.

'Did you find the doctor at home?'

'Yes, he's on his way,' Jim said. 'He's coming round by Lyall Bridge. Has your father woken at all?'

'No,' Kirren said, 'he hasn't stirred.' Still busy with her preparations, she turned her head and glanced at him. 'By the time you've changed those wet clothes, your supper will be ready,' she said.

He went upstairs to his bedroom, changed into dry clothes, and brought the wet ones down with him to dry by the fire. The kitchen was empty; Kirren had gone up to her father again; but his supper was ready on the table: hot mutton broth, thickened with oatmeal, and a loaf of the bread she had baked that day. He sat down to it, gratefully, watched by the tortoiseshell cat, Tibby, who lay in her box beside the hearth with four kittens nestling against her.

When Jim had finished his meal he put on the driest coat he could find, and a hood made from sacks, and went out on a round of the buildings, making sure that all was well with the ewes and lambs quartered there. By then it was past ten o'clock so he walked down the track to meet Dr Hoad, whose temper, when he came, was somewhat short.

'Trust that fool Morris Riddler,' he said, 'to bring me out on a night like this!'

The doctor, having made his examination, stood in front of the bedroom fire and drank the brandy Jim had brought him.

'No bones broken as far as I can tell but I shan't know for certain until he comes to.'

'When do you think that will be?' Kirren asked.

'Can't tell you that. Just don't know. He's pretty badly concussed, of course, but he's got a thick enough skull, God knows, and I doubt if much harm will come of it. Dragged along by his nag, did you say? Yes, that explains the twisted foot. As for the bruising to the head and trunk, well, he'll be pretty sore when he does come round, but maybe that will teach him some sense.'

'What should I do for him when he comes round?'

'Keep him warm and quiet and still, that's all, and if he starts asking for food, give him something easy and light. Gruel, perhaps, or arrowroot. No stimulants, mind! No alcohol! He's had quite enough of that for today.' The doctor drained his brandy-glass. 'I'll come out again some time tomorrow. Not sure when. All depends.'

Jim, having seen the doctor off, returned to Riddler's bedroom. Kirren sat in a chair by the bed with a piece of needlework in her lap. Jim stood looking down at her.

'I'll sit with him now while you get some sleep.'

'I don't need any sleep,' she said. 'You're the one who needs the sleep.'

'Don't argue with me. Just do as I say.'

'No, I will not! Why should I indeed?' Her dark eyes flashed in the candlelight. 'He's *my* father, not yours,' she said.

'I thought you hated him,' Jim said.

'Yes, well, so I do sometimes. Or at least I have done, in the past.' She looked at the grey-faced man in the bed. 'But how can you hate anyone who lies so cold and still and quiet and looks so – so close to death?' she said. 'Oh, he's a selfish, stubborn brute of a man, and I can't pretend I'm fond of him . . . But he's worked so hard all these years, as you know, and for this to happen to him now, when his life has changed for the better at last –'

'He's not going to die,' Jim said.

'Isn't he?'

'No, he is not. What the doctor says is true – your father is as tough as oak. He's a born fighter. You know that.'

'Yes, I know that.'

'Try not to worry. I'm sure there's no need.'

'Very well,' Kirren said. 'But if there's nothing to worry about you may go to your bed and sleep.'

Jim, with a little smile, gave in.

'You'll call me if you need me?' he said.

'Yes, I will, I promise you.'

He touched her arm and left the room.

At five o'clock the following morning, refreshed after more than six hours' sleep, Jim was in the kitchen making tea. During the night the rain had stopped and the outside world seemed strangely still. When he went up to Riddler's room, taking Kirren a cup of tea, she had already drawn the curtains back and there was a cold pale light in the room. His glance went to the man in the bed and he thought he detected some slight change. He turned to Kirren, questioningly, and she gave a nod.

'A short while ago he woke up,' she said. 'It was only for two or three seconds, that's all, and then he closed his eyes again. But he knew me, I'm sure . . .'

174

'Here, drink this while it's hot,' Jim said, and gave her the tea.

He went to the bed and touched Riddler's face. He put his hand in under the bedclothes, felt Riddler's body, and tested his pulse.

'He's a lot warmer than he was last night and I think his pulse is stronger too.'

'Yes, I thought the same myself.'

'He'll soon pick up now.'

'Yes,' she said.

'Have you slept at all?'

'Yes, off and on.'

Jim went down to the kitchen again and drank his own cup of hot sweet tea. Then he went out to the milking-shed and told the men what had happened to Riddler.

'Poor old master,' said Nahum Smith. 'Is he going to be all right?'

'I think so,' Jim said.

'It's certainly some old flood down there. It's like the Sea of Galilee. And the state of the fields as we came down – I've never seen so much mud in my life!'

The miry state of the fields and the yards made extra work for everybody. Because carts could not go on the land, hay and turnips for the sheep sheltering in the pine wood had to be taken up on the horses' backs. Because a trough had overflowed and water had got into the root house, the mangolds all had to be taken out and spread on straw in the barn to dry. And all through the greater part of that day there were similar trials and calamities.

First it was a young sow that fell into an open drain; she was heavily in pig and it took three men to haul her out without doing her any harm. Next it was Bob Lovell who slipped wheeling a barrowload of muck across the fold-yard so that it ran into one of the pillars supporting the linhay and brought part of the roof sagging down. The sheep in the linhay were unharmed but the roof, in danger of further collapse, had to be shored up immediately. Then it was Kirren's pony, Griff, who had to be treated for colic after Willie Townsend had carelessly allowed him to drink from a pail of water just drawn from the well. While Jim was giving the pony a mild draught of peppermint and laudanum, Prue Townsend came to him with a message from Kirren.

'The master's awake and he's asking for you.'

Riddler, clad in a nightshirt now, still lay flat on his back, but there was some colour reviving in his face and he was breathing more normally. Jim sat down in the chair by the bed and Riddler, turning towards him, groaned.

'I ache in every particle,' he said in a low, hoarse voice.

'I'm not surprised,' Jim said, 'after what happened to you.'

'How's my stupid cow of a mare?'

'In better shape than you by far.'

'She doesn't damn well deserve to be, dragging me over the lots like that. Did you bring my saddlebags in?'

'Yes.'

'Money safe?'

'Yes, quite safe.'

'I reckon I'd better leave it to you to pay the men their wages today.'

'Yes, all right,' Jim said. 'They sent their good wishes to you, by the way. They hope you'll soon be on the mend.'

'I hope it myself,' Riddler said.

Kirren came into the room with a bowl of warm barley gruel. Jim helped Riddler to a sitting position and propped him up against his pillows. Kirren sat on the edge of the bed, spread a napkin on Riddler's chest, and offered him a spoonful of gruel. He looked at it with some distaste.

'If this is all I'm getting to eat, the sooner I mend the better,' he said.

Jim, with a little smile for Kirren, quietly left the room.

It was a day of comings and goings; of jobs interrupted and left half done, returned to, and left again; a day of hurriedly eaten meals and short, snatched conversations.

At three o'clock the doctor came and Jim, again called into

the house, was climbing the stairs to Riddler's room when he heard the old man give a bellowing shout. On going in he found Riddler sitting on the edge of the bed, glaring ferociously at the doctor, who stood nearby, quite unmoved.

'He said he couldn't straighten his foot, so I straightened it *for* him,' he explained.

'I reckon the damned fool has just about crippled me for life,' Riddler said.

'Well, we shall see, shan't we?' the doctor said cheerfully, and downstairs, as Kirren and Jim saw him off, he said: 'Keep him in bed for a day or two – if you can get him to stay there. I'll be over again on Tuesday morning.'

Jim went back to the task of cleaning out the root-house, and Kirren, knowing her father was now well enough to be left alone, went to help Prue Townsend in the dairy. It had begun to rain again and by early evening, when Jim paid the men their wages, it was turning to sleet.

'The master's in the best place, tucked up in bed,' said Nahum Smith. 'I shan't be sorry to get there myself and rest my poor old rheumaticky bones.'

When the men had gone Jim went into the barn to look over his ewes and lambs and found Kirren there. She was with her fosterling and was letting him suck her thumb.

'It seems he still remembers me.'

'So he should,' Jim said. 'You were his mother till yesterday.'

'He likes his new mother best.'

They stood for a little while in silence, watching the lamb. Then they both began speaking at once, Kirren to say what a day it had been, and Jim to ask about her father.

'How is he now?'

'Better,' she said. 'But still very quiet – for him.'

'Make the most of it.'

'Yes.' She laughed.

'I told you he would be all right.'

'Yes. You did.'

They left the barn and went into the house and Kirren at once became very busy, first making up the fire and swinging the kettle over it, next moving to and fro, lighting the lamp on the table and setting out the supper things. Jim, having hung up his jacket and hat, stood quietly watching her as she went again and again to the larder, bringing out bread, butter, cheese, and ham, and two or three different kinds of chutney. At last he spoke.

'Kirren, can't you be still for a moment?'

'What?' she said, with a flickering glance. 'Yes, very well, if that's what you want. But I thought you'd be hungry for your supper – .'

'Supper can wait,' Jim said. 'At the moment I want to talk to you and I can't talk sensibly while you keep flitting about like that.'

'Behold me, then – standing still.'

She stood at the opposite side of the table and placed her hands on the back of a chair, folding them there in a gesture of primness. But although she was now facing him, her glance was still evasive, unsure, and, watching her closely in the lamp-light, he saw a faint tinge of colour come stealing slowly into her face.

'Something's been happening to us, hasn't it, during the past few weeks?' he said. And when she failed to answer he said: 'Or perhaps it's only been happening to me?'

'No,' she said, quickly this time, 'it has happened to me as well.'

'Then why won't you look at me, properly?'

'Because – I don't know – it's difficult. And you haven't yet said what it is . . .'

'I love you,' he said, 'and you love me.'

There was a pause. She drew a deep breath.

'You make it all sound so simple,' she said, 'and you're always so – so sure of everything.'

'Kirren, are you afraid of me?'

'No, of course not. Why should I be?'

'I know what you've always felt about men and I'm thinking of what you said to me the day I first came here from Peele – '

'Don't remind me of what I said. That was then. It's different now.'

'How is it different?'

'You know very well.'

She was looking at him directly now, letting him see what she felt for him, and although, when he moved and came towards her, there was a hint of shy alarm in the sudden widening of her eyes, she turned to him and went into his arms and gave herself to him in a kiss that was free of shyness, free of constraint.

In a little while, when Jim spoke again, it was in a voice very quiet and deep, and he looked at her in wonderment, touching her face, her lips, her throat, delicately, with his fingertips.

'When I married you, I was deceived.'

'Who deceived you?'

'You did,' he said. 'You allowed me to think that your past life had roughened you and made you hard, that you had no womanly passion in you, nor any womanly tenderness.'

'And now you know better?' Kirren said.

'Yes,' he said, in the same deep voice, 'now I know you for what you are.'

There came a knock from the room above, loud and peremptory, making them jump. They looked at each other with laughing eyes, drawing apart, reluctantly, with a last lingering touch of the hands.

'That's father,' Kirren said, 'just in case you didn't know.'

'I told you he wouldn't be quiet for long.'

'I'd better go up and see what he wants.'

'I'll come with you.'

'No.'

'Why not?'

'I don't want you with me. Not just yet. He'd know there was something – he'd see too much.'

'No one would ever see anything that you didn't want them to see,' Jim said. 'Not if you had made up your mind to it.'

'You think so, do you? I'm not so sure. And I don't intend to take any chances until I've had time to – to gather my wits.'

Another loud knock and she hurried away. The kitchen seemed suddenly empty and bare. Jim stood, a faint smile on his lips, listening to the sounds overheard, of Kirren and her father talking together. Then, in a moment, she reappeared.

'He's asking for something to eat,' she said, 'and he wants you to take it up to him.'

When Jim entered the bedroom, with a bowl of gruel and milk on a tray, Riddler was sitting up in bed.

'Is this all I get? Pig-slops again?' he said, as he received the tray.

'H'mm,' Jim said, surveying him, 'you are better, obviously.'

'Yes, if you thought to be rid of me, you'll have to wait a while longer yet.' Riddler motioned him to a chair. 'Meanwhile you can sit and talk and watch me feasting myself,' he said.

Later, Jim and Kirren ate their own supper, sitting opposite one another at the kitchen table, in the golden circle of light from the lamp.

With the curtains drawn close over the windows, against the cold wet night outside, and a good fire burning red on the hearth, they were shut in together in comfort and warmth and because they had the kitchen to themselves and sat there together in strange new special intimacy, the room seemed somehow to take something from them, of wonderment and discovery, and to give it back again in waves.

Knowing that Riddler was now asleep, they talked together in quiet voices, and everything they said to each other deepened the intimate feeling between them.

'If we were not already married, would you marry me?'

'Yes, of course.'

'Ours was a strange wedding,' he said. 'Surely no other two people can ever have married in such a way, knowing nothing about one another, caring nothing, as we did then.' And after a little while he said: 'When did you first find it had changed? That you could care for me after all?'

'I don't know,' Kirren said, 'and I don't think I'd tell you if I did.'

'I would tell *you*, if I knew,' he said.

'But you don't know?'

'No, not quite.'

' "During the past few weeks." – That's what you said a while ago.'

'I think, with me, it's been longer than that.'

'And with me,' Kirren said.

'Your father said this would happen to us . . . that nature was bound to play its part . . . that a man and a woman thrown together were bound to feel something for each other sooner or later.'

'I know pretty well what my father said. But oh, Jim, is that all it is?' She looked at him in laughing dismay. 'Something that would have happened to us, quite regardless of who we were? Just any woman? Any man? I can't believe that.'

'No more can I. Because you are not just any woman and I am not just any man. But perhaps in some peculiar way your father sensed something about us, or perhaps it was just pure chance. Anyway, however it was, he was in the right of it.'

There was a silence. He looked at her.

'Kirren,' he said.

'Yes, what?'

'Your father is much better now. I don't think it will be necessary for you to sit up with him tonight.'

'No,' she said. 'I don't think it will.' She looked at him with dark, steady gaze. 'Tonight will be our wedding night.'

In another three days Riddler was up and about again, groaning and swearing at the pain in his joints, but hobbling stubbornly everywhere, refusing all help save that of a walking-stick. First he went to see his mare in her stall, to give her a piece of his mind, he said, and let her see what she'd done to him. Next he went to look at the fields, which were still badly waterlogged, and the valley meadows down below, where the floods still lay like a great shallow lake. And lastly, sighting the doctor riding slowly up the track, he went hobbling down to meet him.

'Tell me, do I look as if I need you?' he asked. 'No, by God, I'm damned if I do!' But almost in the same breath he said: 'Ah, well, having come this far, you'd better come in and have a drink, I suppose.'

The weather continued wet and cold and the valley lots remained flooded for the best part of ten days. Slowly, at last, the floodwater drained away from the meadows and the green springing grass was seen again, but everywhere, both in meadows and fields, the land was kept wet by repeated rains.

'Is there to be no end to it?' Kirren said. 'Are we never to be dry again?'

'You needn't go out in it,' Riddler said. 'Being a woman, you're lucky like that. You can stay snug and warm in your kitchen here and pretend to be busy about your chores.'

'And what about my dairywork? And going to market once a week? I have to go out of doors sometimes, otherwise I should suffocate. But oh, dear, what wouldn't I give to have a few dry days for a change!'

'You seem cheerful enough, anyway, in spite of the weather,' Riddler said.

'Do I?' said Kirren, on her guard.

It was one morning after breakfast, and she and her father were alone. Jim was out tending his flock but Riddler, whose joints were still troubling him, was taking it easy by the fire.

'Not only cheerful, neither,' he said, 'but something else as well besides.'

Kirren, at the table, washing up, glanced at him from under her lashes, but made no reply, and Riddler, in a thoughtful tone, went on:

'I can't quite fathom it out, but there's something different about you these days. I've noticed it once or twice of late, but I don't just know what it is, unless it's something you've done to your hair.'

'My hair is the same as it has been for years.'

'Then maybe you're wearing a new dress,' he said.

'This is the dress I bought last spring.'

182

'Well, it's a mystery, then, that's all, and I shall have to give it up. But there *is* a difference in you all the same and whatever it is it suits you right well.'

'Does it, now? Fancy that.'

Kirren now came to the hearth to fetch a cloth for drying up, plucking it down from the string line that hung in a loop from the mantelpiece. Instead of turning away, however, she stood with the cloth between her hands, and Riddler, leaning back in his chair, slowly raised his face to hers.

For a little while father and daughter eyed each other, glimmeringly, until the amused satisfaction of one and the indulgent mockery of the other kindled a mutual gleam of warmth mixed with a kind of sardonic understanding. Riddler was the first to speak.

'I knew you'd come to it in the end.'

'Then no doubt you're feeling well pleased with yourself.'

'It seems I'm not the only one . . . '

'I suppose you think the credit's all yours?'

'Of course the credit is all mine! Damn it, girl, if it wasn't for me you'd still be the same crabby spinster you were before, sharp-tongued and hard as nails, all back-answers and black looks and temper enough for two or three!'

'No compliments, please,' Kirren said.

'You were made for marriage, Kirrie. I always knew that, all along. And I'll tell you something else as well – you were made to be the mother of sons.'

'All in good time,' she said, 'perhaps.'

'Time!' he said, glaring at her. 'You've already wasted a year and a half! Yes, and that reminds me, while we are speaking of such matters – next time you go in to town, buy yourself a double bed, so that Jim can sleep with you, decently, as a husband should, instead of creeping about at night, robbing a poor old man of his sleep with all this opening and shutting of doors.'

A few days afterwards news came to Godsakes, via one of the carters at Peele, that Philip Sutton's wife Jane had given birth to a baby son.

'Well,' Riddler said to Jim and Kirren, 'I never thought to say such a thing about the Suttons, but let that be an example to you.'

Chapter Twelve

The spring and summer of that year were the coldest and wettest anyone could remember and the bad conditions brought much trouble to farmers everywhere.

In the second lambing at Godsakes, losses were almost as bad as in the first, and all through the summer there was much to do to keep the flock free of foot-rot and sickness. It was the same with the rest of the stock: a constant watch had to be kept on the cattle and at the slightest hint of a cough or a chill Jim was in close attendance, rubbing the beasts down with a brush to invigorate them, and administering soothing drinks. Even so they lost one of their best cows from pleuro-pneumonia; also a heifer fifteen months old.

There was no proper course with the crops that year. Everything happened out of turn. Swedes and mangolds could not be sown until the first week in June, and carrots were sown later still. They made growth quickly enough but so did the weeds, and with the land so sticky and wet, little hoeing could be done. Three acres of Dutch beans were spoilt by mildew; they had to be cut down while green and fed to the pigs; and haymaking, begun in June, was still in progress at the end of August.

But whatever the trials and anxieties of that dismal year it seemed as though some benign spirit was keeping watch over Godsakes Farm and its people. There was a radiance over their lives; a sense of warm unity in everything they did together; an optimism at work in them that neither anxiety nor misfortune could touch.

Jim had the feeling, new every day, that his life was rather astonishing, and that many great and marvellous gifts had been bestowed upon him. He had always been an ambitious man; had always felt that he could do great things; but now this feeling had another dimension, as though he saw his future life laid out before him, as in a vision, with a rich golden light spread over it. Problems were nothing; he welcomed them; for he felt with utter certainty that he could overcome them all; that he had it in him to mould his life pretty much as he chose. And at the heart of this feeling of his, giving him this special faith, was the love that had grown between him and Kirren.

'Sometimes I feel that I don't deserve the good fortune that's come my way,' he said to her once, 'but I mean to deserve it, in the future, by working for it and earning it.'

'When did you not work?' Kirren said. 'You have always worked, all your life.'

'All that is nothing,' he said with a smile, 'to what I shall do in future years.'

At the end of August, when haymaking was finished at last, they cut their few acres of dredge-corn, oats and barley as before. But this year, due to the constant rain, both barley and oats were spoilt by disease, which meant that the whole crop was fit only for the pigs and fowls.

'God! Just look at it!' Riddler said, holding a sodden, discoloured sheaf aloft on the prongs of his hay-fork. 'Did you ever see such stuff? It'll never be dry in a hundred years!' And as September came in, with the weather still wet and cold, he said: 'I've never known such a summer as this and I never want to see another like it again so long as I live.'

The only comfort Riddler could find for the year's disappointments was that things had been much worse at Peele. Abelard's losses at lambing time had been almost half as great again as Jim's and there had been further losses since. Among the pedigree Alderneys that were such a source of pride at Peele there had been an outbreak of rinder-pest, and ten prize-winning cows had been lost, together with a number of calves. And, even worse than this, for a farm that grew so much corn, was the weather's effect on their harvest.

Their spring corn had never been sown, due to the wet and the cold, and except for a growth of green weeds, many fields remained bare all through the summer and into autumn. And their winter corn was a sorry sight: acres and acres of wheat and barley laid low by the wind and the rain, the barley sprouting in the ear, the wheat so infected with the smut that whole fields were darkened by it. There was no golden glow in the harvest fields at Peele that year, but only a sombre, shadowy pall. There was no happy noise of reaping-machines, for the corn was so wet and so badly lodged that it all had to be cut by hand.

'Just look at them all, swarming about!' Riddler said to Kirren and Jim. 'They're having to put their backs into it and do a bit of work for a change! And their masters won't make three thousand pounds from their harvest this year, by God! They'll be lucky if they make three thousand pence! This damned wet season has hit them a sight harder than it's hit us here. It makes me laugh like a spinning-top to see them slaving away over there, knowing they'll get no gain from it.'

'Why, what good does that do us?' Kirren said.

'I don't know what it does for *you* but it does *me* a power of good to see bad luck come to them for a change.'

It was a dull but dry day and they were at work in their own harvest field, opening up the corn-shocks, soaked by previous days of rain, and setting the sheaves out in twos so that they might dry in the wind. Kirren and Jim were working together, separating the wet sheaves, and Riddler, who had finished his row, was standing near them, his hands on his hips, looking across the valley at Peele.

'After what they did to me I reckon I'm about entitled to crow over them for a change,' he said.

'And do you intend,' Kirren asked, 'to carry your grudge right through to the end of your life?'

187

'Yes, why shouldn't I?' Riddler said.

'It seems to me rather childish, that's all.'

'Childish, is it?'

'Yes,' Kirren said. 'It was all a long time ago. It's silly to bear a grudge for so long. Jim doesn't feel like that. He's put his quarrel out of his mind.'

'Has he, now?'

'Yes, he has.'

'And what's so surprising about that?' Riddler said with a curl of his lip. 'What was his quarrel compared with mine? The harm he got at the Suttons' hands was nothing but a fleabite compared with the harm they did me. In fact it was a bit of good luck for him when John Sutton turned him out, for he wouldn't have come to us otherwise and how else, in God's name, would he ever have got a farm of his own? He's fallen on his feet and no mistake, and well he knows it, you may be sure.'

With his chin jutting pugnaciously, Riddler turned and went stumping off, to work by himself on a row of shocks some little way further down the field. Jim and Kirren, having stopped work, looked at each other across the sheaves.

'It's no good trying to change him, you know. His hatred for Sutton goes too deep.'

'Yes, I know, I know,' Kirren said. 'I'd do better to hold my tongue, I know.'

'Nor is it any good holding me up as an example of Christian charity because what your father says is true – I *have* fallen on my feet and I am well aware of it. Indeed, it is a very strange thing, but twice in my life so far, when someone has done me a bad turn, it has worked out to my advantage in the end. First, when my uncle abandoned me and John Sutton took me in, and then, as your father just said, when John Sutton turned me out and I came over here.'

'You consider yourself lucky, it seems.'

'Yes, I do, for I've not only got this farm but I've got you as well.'

'Riches indeed!' Kirren said.

'Oh, you may mock if you like, looking at me with those dark gipsy eyes! But what more could a man want from life?'

'Surely, if you give it some thought, there must be something more you want . . .'

'Kirren, are you telling me something?'

'Yes. I'm going to have a child.'

They stood looking at one another and there was a quietness over them both. A stillness in him. A growing smile.

'Well, that explains it,' he said at last.

'Explains what?'

'Why you are looking so beautiful.'

'Am I beautiful?'

'Yes. You are.'

'I take it you're pleased, then, with my news?'

'You don't need to ask me that.'

'My father is looking over at us. He will be shouting at us in a minute, asking why we are standing idle.'

'In that case, we'd better get on.'

They resumed their work in unison, taking the wet sheaves from the shock, shaking the raindrops out of them, and standing them up, two by two, in the path of the wind.

In another few minutes, however, they stopped work again because overhead in the grey sky the clouds parted and the sun shone out, falling on them with a gentle warmth and filling the valley with a soft bright light. They stood with their faces upturned to the sun, grateful for the light and the warmth they had seen and felt so rarely that summer, and Riddler, just a little way off, stood in exactly the same way, lifting his blunt, crooked face to the sun in a childlike gesture of gratitude.

And away on the far side of the valley the reapers in the fields at Peele, labouring over their blighted harvest, also stopped work and stood, greeting the sun with a little cheer that was heard clearly in the fields at Godsakes. Hearing the sound of this cheer, Kirren and Jim smiled at each other, and Kirren, putting one hand to her eyes, turned to look out over the valley, softly lit by the golden sun shining through the parted clouds.

'I wonder how this valley will look, and these two farms,

189

when our children are growing up, say in ten or twenty years' time.'

'You are looking a long way ahead.'

'Yes, and why not?' Kirren said.

SEEDTIME AND HARVEST

Mary E. Pearce

Linn Mercybright had survived the Depression years and the slur of an illegitimate son. When gentle easygoing Charlie Truscott proposed marriage it seemed that she might at last know the taste of happiness.

But trouble lay ahead when a surprised inheritance enabled Linn to buy a farm. The serenity of their marriage became ruffled by her stubborn determination to run things her way. Charlie seemed to spend all his time helping pretty fragile Mrs Shaw on the neighbouring farm, and the advent of World War II was to cause further anguish with the departure of her cherished son . . .

In SEEDTIME AND HARVEST Mary Pearce brings to a triumphant conclusion her powerful saga of English farming life.

'Sheer country magic'
James Herriot

Futura Publications
Fiction
0 7088 2965 1

All Futura Books are available at your bookshop or
newsagent, or can be ordered from the following address:
Futura Books, Cash Sales Department,
P.O. Box 11, Falmouth, Cornwall.

Please send cheque or postal order (no currency), and
allow 55p for postage and packing for the first book
plus 22p for the second book and 14p for each additional
book ordered up to a maximum charge of £1.75 in U.K.

Customers in Eire and B.F.P.O. please allow 55p for
the first book, 22p for the second book plus 14p per
copy for the next 7 books, thereafter 8p per book.

Overseas customers please allow £1 for postage and
packing for the first book and 25p per copy for each
additional book.